SHORT AMERICAN THRILLERS

Edited by Rebecca K. Rizzo

The Globe Pequot Press

Guilford, Connecticut

Previously published as *Campfire Thrillers: The Short and Scary Ones*

"You Must Flee Again" by Paul Spencer is reprinted with permission of Forrest J Ackerman.

"The Open Window" appeared originally in *The Short Stories of Saki (H. H. Munro)*, copyright © 1930, published by The Viking Press, Inc., New York.

"The Considerate Hosts" by Thorp McClusky, copyright © 1939, is reprinted with permission of Weird Tales, Ltd.

"Faces" by Arthur J. Burks, copyright © 1966, is reprinted with permission of Forrest J Ackerman.

Library of Congress Cataloging-in-Publication Data

Short and scary thrillers /
 Short and scary thrillers / edited by Rebecca K. Rizzo.
  p. cm.
 Previuosly published under title: Campfire thrillers : the short and scary ones.
 ISBN 0-7627-0319-9 (alk. paper)
 1. Ghost stories. I. Rizzo, Rebecca K.
PN6120.95.G45C36 1999
808.83'8733--DC21   98-20581
                                                 CIP

Cover design by Maryann Dubé
Illustrations by Maryann Dubé

♻ This book is printed on recycled paper.
Manufactured in the United States of America
Revised Edition/Nineth Printing

CONTENTS

ABOUT THE EDITOR

Rebecca K. Rizzo's camping career officially ended when her occupied tent was mauled by a North American brown grizzly on the Upper Peninsula of Michigan. Now content reading and editing scary stories rather than living them, she has sought out the safer life of a computer marketing executive in Charlotte, North Carolina, where she lives with her husband, David, and two sons.

INTRODUCTION

Well, you're off. The weekend camping trip is upon you and the packing has begun: packs, sleeping bags, tents, food, and, of course, ghost stories. No camping trip is complete without the appropriate repertoire of ghastly stories told in the glow of the campfire. All the better if there is a chill in the air and an unaccountable rustle in the trees on a still night. Your imagination will turn the best ghost stories into chilling reality. You won't want to be alone in your tent. In fact, I advise against it.

Short and Scary Thrillers was created for people who love traditional ghost stories while camping (or for those who prefer to be haunted in front of the fire at home). Stories of the twisted, the macabre, and the unexpected will frighten even the stoutest of heart at night, in the woods around the campfire. This collection, in its compact size, will be easy to take along and will keep your heart racing and your palms clammy.

My fun came from trying out hundreds of stories in search of the most unsettling few, which appear in this group. Most of the stories are traditional in nature. You will not find stories about mad scientists, robots, or werewolves in the pages that follow. If you read carefully, though, you will find plenty to guarantee an uneasy night's sleep.

I hope you enjoy these stories, whether around the campfire or in your living room. Beware, however. Many believe these stories to be true. Let your nerves be the judge.

RKR

YOU MUST FLEE AGAIN

Paul Spencer

Sometimes I think the Fates must have a rather ironical sense of humor. Take the case of the stranger who broke into my home last fall.

It was my housekeeper's night off, poor woman; rain had started at dusk, and she had gone out into the downpour with a noticeable lack of enthusiasm. For some time after her departure, I sat alone by the fire, feeling very snug as I listened to the swish and spatter of the raindrops, driven splashing against the windows by a gale of almost malignant fury. Anyone abroad in that deluge must have been thoroughly miserable. But not necessarily—terrified.

Terrified is exactly what the little man was. My door—unlocked—gave clicking sounds as he frantically tried its knob, rousing me from my reverie. He staggered in and shut the door with careful soundlessness; turning, he faced me as I twisted in my chair to see who had entered. He jumped, but his expression did not change; it remained one of blind, maddened fear.

As I looked him over, I was reminded of a frightened mouse. He was a small, thin fellow—and his tired-looking face was so expressive of helpless misery and terror that it was half tragic and half absurd. He wore no hat, and his hair was sleek with rain; grey locks were clinging damply to his forehead. He trembled—and the night was not that cold. For a long moment, neither of us spoke; he was gasping, apparently from running. Finally he panted, "I beg your pardon—I—may—may I stay here a while?"

Then he staggered to a chair and collapsed into it. I couldn't hold back a scowl; his soaked clothes must be ruining the upholstery. Why hadn't he worn a raincoat. The scowl went unnoticed; his mind seemed to be elsewhere.

He looked up at me timidly. "I know this must seem strange," he gasped. "Dreadful imposition. But I—I got caught in the storm you see."

I returned his gaze coldly. "In that case, what's wrong with my very spacious front porch? Better be honest with me; what are you up to? Police after you?"

He sat looking at me piteously, his gasps gradually quieting.

I stood up. "Well, go ahead. What's your story?"

He gulped miserably. "Oh, I can explain. It's not the police. It's all perfectly—I mean, I—" His gaze fell to the floor, and he regarded the rug for a while in silence. Then he quivered, as though from a sudden chill, and looked sharply at the windows. "Would—would you be good enough to draw the shades?"

I scowled; the request seemed both odd and presumptuous. Nevertheless, I humored him, and pulled down the shades; he relaxed noticeably. With folded arms, I stared down at him severely. "Go ahead," I repeated.

He licked his lips and brushed the damp hair back from his forehead; then he told me his story:

"All this will seem incredible, I suppose, but it's God's truth, sir. I wouldn't be here otherwise. If I were just a—a prowler, say, would I have come in the front door? Well—

"I'm an antique repair man in one of the big galleries in town.

I live by myself in a little apartment; a couple of miles from here, it must be. I've never been in any kind of trouble before this; I'm a quiet man, living a routine sort of life—at least, I was.

"Well, I'd been living here uneventfully for almost twenty years. Then something happened that upset my whole existence. Mentally as well as physically.

"One night coming home from work I was pretty deep in thought about one thing or another; so wrapped up in myself that I didn't notice when the bus got to my stop. When I realized what had happened, I was a good mile out of my way. I got off at the next stop. It was a bracing sort of night, so I decided to walk back, rather than take a bus.

"The neighborhood was unfamiliar—I'd never been out that way before. I strolled along rather slowly, giving my surroundings a leisurely examination. As I walked, dusk fell, and the streetlights came on. The semi-darkness gave the houses around me a some-what—*eerie* look. You see, it was an old section of town, and I suppose most of the residents had moved to more convenient parts of the city. Anyhow, many of the houses were empty, even boarded up. Some of them suggested the 'haunted houses' I remember fearing as a child.

"I wasn't really uneasy, you understand—I'm not a particularly imaginative man; but the atmosphere was there. So it came as something of a shock when, in the long rows of dingy abandoned houses, I saw a thin line of light. It peeped through a crack in the boards over a tightly nailed-up window, in a building that seemed dilapidated beyond repair.

"I stopped in front of that window—it gave on the street—and I gazed at it with a good deal of puzzlement. The other windows were boarded so tight I couldn't tell whether there was light in any of the other rooms or not; but this particular window had this small crack in the boards over it, and light gleamed through. As I watched, the crack *blinked* at me. That is, it went dark for an instant, then lit up again. It occurred to me that such a phenomenon might be caused by someone's walking in front of the window, inside. And it seemed odd.

"Now, as I say, I'm not an imaginative man—and not usually inquisitive, either. Still, that light and its blinking—it did it again—set me to thinking the matter over. And it irritated me, because I couldn't quite understand it. What would anyone be doing in a boarded-up old house, and at that hour? Well, I felt I had to know the answer. I looked up and down the street—rather guiltily, I suppose. Then, seeing no one in sight, I entered the house's yard.

"I grabbed the window-ledge with my finger-tips and gave a little jump. I couldn't hold myself up there, but as I bobbed by the crack, I caught a glimpse of part of the room within. As I hit the ground again, I was trembling.

"It wasn't the sort of room you'd expect to find in an abandoned house. Just with that fleeting glimpse, I'd received a distinct impression of immaculate cleanness; not whiteness, but a gleaming, polished *black*. I'd never seen a room with shining black walls before, and somehow—it frightened me. It seemed unnatural, perverse. Moreover, I'd glimpsed part of a human figure, and it was garbed as though for a costume ball. Scarlet with black figurings. Something in the design disturbed me, but I hadn't been able to get a good look at it; just a swift impression of part of a red-and-black robed back, and shining black walls.

"I stood there in the deepening twilight, shivering, and thinking the matter over. No explanation came to me, but I told myself there could be no justification for the sudden fright that glimpse had given me. There must be some ordinary, common-sense explanation. But in any case, I felt I had to know."

At this point the little man looked around him rather furtively, and gazed with particular intentness at the shaded windows. Then his glance fell to the floor again, and he resumed his narration. I stood leaning against the arm of my chair, and noncommittally regarded my fingernails.

"Well," he went on, "there was a battered old orange-crate lying on the lawn—it was a pretty shabby neighborhood, you see—and I stood it on end under the window and climbed up for a good long look. It was hard to see much through the crack, and I had to fill in with my imagination the half-forms and half-gestures I saw. To this day I can't be sure just what it was I observed.

"There seemed to be only one person in the room, a man of rather unusual height, clothed—as I said—in a crimson robe, with enigmatic designs in black. When I looked this second time, the man was kneeling near the center of the room, and making very curious gestures which I could see only in part. A foot or so beyond the man, something I couldn't see was giving off a weirdly multi-colored smoke which writhed and eddied like a concourse of rainbow-hued snakes. The man seemed to be mumbling to himself, a faint drone which suggested no words in any language I'd ever heard.

"The scene was so utterly bizarre, so unaccountable in terms of human life as I knew it, that I was fascinated, and stayed perched on the box—staring for dear life, and hoping I'd see something which would explain it all. I suppose I would have looked very suspicious to any passer-by; but none came, or at least none disturbed me.

"How long I remained there staring I have no idea. It must have been hours. Very little seemed to happen, at least very little that was even remotely intelligible. The gestures and faint mumbling went on a long while, then ceased, and the colored smoke eddied and whirled for an instant, as though a draft had entered the room. At about this point I became aware that the red-robed man was not alone in the room as I had thought; there was another man, similarly robed but with black the predominating color, and red that of the designs. There was something strange, almost unhuman, in the posture and movements of this new figure.

"The actions of the two from then on were beyond all relevance to anything I know. They spoke from time to time, but always softly, and the syllables never resolved into any intelligible words. Moreover, the more I watched the less sure I was of the number—and sex—of the people in the room. The fragmentary glimpses I had were most confusing and—disconcerting.

"Finally I noticed that the mumblings of the strange persons were now accompanied by a semi-musical droning which rose and fell as though with the accents of speech; and the single person I now saw stood in profile, silent, in an attitude of respectful listening. A shadow fell upon him. My scalp prickled with a sense of approaching menace; I shifted my weight uneasily on my aching legs. The box creaked, sharply.

"The man in the room turned his head and stared straight into my eyes."

Here, again, the stranger paused. Once more he glanced around, and he moved restlessly in the chair.

"Go on!" I urged, rather severely.

The little man sighed, and continued:

"There was no question but that he saw me—or, rather, saw my eyes at the slit. His face writhed in a most extraordinary expression—a mingling of utter panic and the most intense and shocking malignancy. He moved, swiftly—and so did I.

"I dropped to the ground, terrified, and ran. I was hardly out of the yard when, glancing back in fright, I saw the whole slab of boards over the window moving outward. It was held by the man in the black-figured scarlet robe, who instantly saw me and shouted something hoarse and unintelligible. The light in the room went out as he spoke.

"All the way to the apartment-house I ran, and I ran up the

stairs to my floor, and down the hall to my apartment. Once in the room, panting and covered with sweat, I locked the door and remained standing for a long time, quivering in fear. Finally I relaxed a bit and got up enough courage to go to bed; but I slept little that night. Or since.

"For it didn't end there. Rather, that glimpse—I of them, and they of me—was only the beginning. The days were getting shorter as autumn came on; when it began to be dusk by the time I got home, I noticed that I would be followed from the bus-stop to my home. Whoever followed did so at a distance, and in shadow, but after the first couple of nights the creature's purpose was plain enough. I was being hunted. Someone wanted to—to get me alone somewhere in the dark, where nobody could see us, and—well, what he would do I preferred not to think.

"I was especially careful, of course, never to go beyond my stop on the bus-line; and it occurred to me before long to take a different route home. At first the prowler, or prowlers, missed me on the new route; but after two nights of freedom, I saw someone dodge into the shadows as I turned to look.

"It was a vague, unnameable menace, but it was terrifying enough. My mind was never easy, and I dreaded the end of each working day. My work suffered, and I was spoken to rather harshly more than once, but how could I explain? I was convinced, you see, that whatever it was I had seen, its perpetrators were resolved that my half-knowledge should never be imparted, and they were out to destroy me. Moreover, I had no idea who—or what—they were, nor whether their normal residence was in that old house, nor whether they dwelt together or separately. I wouldn't be likely to recognize them again, dressed in ordinary clothes. I could know them only by their actions.

"Finally, they struck. One night I tried another new route, through a neighborhood with which I wasn't overly familiar. To my alarm, I found that I had to go through a long, dead-black alley-way to get to my street. Well, I feared going around the old way more than I feared the alley, so I went ahead.

"What a horrible few moments that was! I went through slowly, feeling my way, breathing cautiously, and tensed for I didn't know what. But I got to the other end of the alley, and let out my breath in a great sigh of relief—when something *past which I had walked* struck at me from behind.

"I was walking as the blow fell, and had just quickened my pace; which must be the reason why the blow only grazed the back of my head. I reeled, momentarily blinded with shock and pain. Then, quite automatically and without conscious thought save pure terror, I recovered my balance and ran madly, spurred by anguish and panic.

"I have no memory of getting back to my room; my mind simply blacked out. All I remember is that as I turned to enter the door of the building, I glimpsed my assailant, not pursuing me at all, but standing—rather oddly hunched, I thought—at the mouth of the alley, motionless. Once safely in my room, I examined the back of my head with the aid of two mirrors, and found that my hair was lightly splashed with blood at the roots, from a series of parallel scratches. These were only superficial, though, and had already stopped bleeding. Still, I looked at those scratches for a long time. My assailant must have used a most extraordinary sort of weapon.

"That was last night. This morning I was afraid to leave my room; but the bright sun finally dispelled the worst of my fears, and I went to work. When it came time to go home, I was dismayed to find the sky so overcast that the evening was completely dark. After a good deal of troubled thought, I decided to take my usual route home, since the walk from the bus-stop was shorter than the walks necessary on the other routes. But I fidgeted a good deal all during the bus-ride.

"As I stepped off the bus, the rain started; and I thought I saw something hiding behind a phone-pole a few yards from me. As the bus drove off, my fear was realized: a dark shape stepped from behind the pole, one arm upraised.

"I turned and ran, blindly, in the first direction that suggested itself. A figure stepped into my path—friend or foe I never found out, for I dodged with panicky swiftness and ran in another direction, ran with hysterical speed, the rain driving hard into my face. My hat flew off, and in confusion I slowed an instant—only to dash on faster than before, when I heard close behind me the quick tread of pursuing feet.

"I twisted and turned, up one street and down another, splashing wildly through puddles, elbowing occasional pedestrians, dodging cars, completely out of my mind with fear. I ran for blocks and blocks—all the pent-up terror of weeks let loose in a blind burst of energy. It was like a nightmare; I had no idea where I was going or why—except to escape my nameless pursuer. The thought of finding a policeman came to me, abruptly, but I was in an out-of-the-way part of the residential district, and passed few people, including no policemen. Finally, as I ran, out of my mental turmoil came the idea of taking refuge in a house—any house—and I ran to this one."

He stopped, and looked at me beseechingly. "He—or they—may be lurking outside. I don't dare to leave. You *must* keep me here, at least until morning! Don't you see my position? Surely you'll help me!"

He looked very pathetic as he pleaded. But—

"I'm sorry," I said evenly, "but I'm afraid you've come to the wrong person. It's hardly strange, of course; there are—quite a few of us." I flexed my hands, unsheathing my claws.

He had time for just one short scream.

THE KIT-BAG

Algernon Blackwood

When the words 'Not Guilty' sounded through the crowded courtroom that dark December afternoon, Arthur Wilbraham, the great criminal KC, and leader for the triumphant defence, was represented by his junior; but Johnson, his private secretary, carried the verdict across to his chambers like lightning.

'It's what we expected, I think,' said the barrister, without emotion; 'and, personally, I am glad the case is over.' There was no particular sign of pleasure that his defence of John Turk, the murderer, on a plea of insanity, had been successful, for no doubt he felt, as everybody who had watched the case felt, that no man had ever better deserved the gallows.

'I'm glad too,' said Johnson. He had sat in the court for ten days watching the face of the man who had carried out with callous detail one of the most brutal and cold-blooded murders of recent years.

The counsel glanced up at his secretary. They were more than employer and employed; for family and other reasons, they were friends. 'Ah, I remember; yes,' he said with a kind smile, 'and you want to get away for Christmas? You're going to skate and ski in the Alps, aren't you? If I was your age I'd come with you.'

Johnson laughed shortly. He was a young man of twenty-six, with a delicate face like a girl's. 'I can catch the morning boat now,' he said; 'but that's not the reason I'm glad the trial is over. I'm glad it's over because I've seen the last of that man's dreadful face. It positively haunted me. That white skin, with the black hair brushed low over the forehead, is a thing I shall never forget, and the description of the way the dismembered body was crammed and packed with lime into that ——'

'Don't dwell on it, my dear fellow,' interrupted the other, looking at him curiously out of his keen eyes, 'don't think about it. Such pictures have a trick of coming back when one least wants them.' He paused a moment. 'Now go,' he added presently, 'and enjoy your holiday. I shall want all your energy for my Parliamentary work when you get back. And don't break your neck skiing.'

Johnson shook hands and took his leave. At the door he turned suddenly.

'I knew there was something I wanted to ask you,' he said. 'Would you mind lending me one of your kit-bags? It's too late to get one tonight, and I leave in the morning before the shops are open.'

'Of course; I'll send Henry over with it to your rooms. You shall have it the moment I get home.'

'I promise to take great care of it,' said Johnson gratefully, delighted to think that within thirty hours he would be nearing the brilliant sunshine of the high Alps in winter. The thought of that criminal court was like an evil dream in his mind.

He dined at his club and went on to Bloomsbury, where he occupied the top floor in one of those old, gaunt houses in which the rooms are large and lofty. The floor below his own was vacant and unfurnished, and below that were other lodgers whom he did not know. It was cheerless, and he looked forward heartily to a change. That night was even more cheerless: it was miserable, and few people were about. A cold, sleety rain was driving down the streets before the keenest east wind he had ever felt. It howled dismally among the big, gloomy houses of the great squares, and when he reached his rooms he heard it whistling and shouting over the world of black roofs beyond his windows.

In the hall he met his landlady, shading a candle from the draughts with her thin hand. 'This come by a man from Mr Wilbr'im's, sir.'

She pointed to what was evidently the kit-bag, and Johnson thanked her and took it upstairs with him. 'I shall be going abroad in the morning for ten days, Mrs Monks,' he said. 'I'll leave an address for letters.'

'And I hope you'll 'ave a merry Christmas, sir,' she said, in a raucous, wheezy voice that suggested spirits, 'and better weather than this.'

'I hope so too,' replied her lodger, shuddering a little as the wind went roaring down the street outside.

When he got upstairs he heard the sleet volleying against the window panes. He put his kettle on to make a cup of hot coffee, and then set about putting a few things in order for his absence. 'And now I must pack—such as my packing is,' he laughed to himself, and set to work at once.

He liked the packing, for it brought the snow mountains so vividly before him, and made him forget the unpleasant scenes of the past ten days. Besides, it was not elaborate in nature. His friend had lent him the very thing—a stout canvas kit-bag, sack-shaped, with holes round the neck for the brass bar and padlock. It was a bit shapeless, true, and not much to look at, but its capacity was unlimited, and there was no need to pack carefully. He shoved in his waterproof coat, his fur cap and gloves, his skates and climbing boots, his sweaters, snowboots, and ear-caps; and then on the top of these he piled his woollen shirts and underwear, his thick socks, puttees, and knickerbockers. The dress suit came next, in case the hotel people dressed for dinner, and then, thinking of the best way to pack his white shirts, he paused a moment to reflect. 'That's the worst of these kit-bags,' he mused vaguely, standing in the centre of the sitting-room, where he had come to fetch some string.

It was after ten o'clock. A furious gust of wind rattled the windows as though to hurry him up, and he thought with pity of the poor Londoners whose Christmas would be spent in such a climate, whilst he was skimming over snowy slopes in bright sunshine, and dancing in the evening with rosy-cheeked girls—Ah! that reminded him; he must put in his dancing-pumps and evening socks. He crossed over from his sitting-room to the cupboard on the landing where he kept his linen.

And as he did so he heard someone coming softly up the stairs.

He stood still a moment on the landing to listen. It was Mrs Monks's step, he thought; she must be coming up with the last post. But then the steps ceased suddenly, and he heard no more. They were at least two flights down, and he came to the conclusion they were too heavy to be those of his bibulous landlady. No doubt they belonged to a late lodger who had mistaken his floor. He went into his bedroom and packed his pumps and dress-shirts as best he could.

The kit-bag by this time was two-thirds full, and stood upright on its own base like a sack of flour. For the first time he noticed that it was old and dirty, the canvas faded and worn, and that it had obviously been subjected to rather rough treatment. It was not a very nice bag to have sent him—certainly not a new one, or one that his chief valued. He gave the matter a passing thought, and went on with his packing. Once or twice, however, he caught himself wondering who it could have been wandering down below, for Mrs Monks had not come up with letters, and the floor was empty and unfurnished. From time to time, moreover, he was almost certain he heard a soft tread of someone padding about over the bare boards—cautiously, stealthily, as silently as possible—and, further, that the sounds had been lately coming distinctly nearer.

For the first time in his life he began to feel a little creepy. Then, as though to emphasize this feeling, an odd thing happened: as he left the bedroom, having just packed his recalcitrant white shirts, he noticed that the top of the kit-bag lopped over towards him with an extraordinary resemblance to a human face. The canvas fell into a fold like a nose and forehead, and the brass rings for the padlock just filled the position of the eyes. A shadow—or was it a travel stain? for he could not tell exactly—looked like hair. It gave him rather a turn, for it was so absurdly, so outrageously, like the face of John Turk, the murderer.

He laughed, and went into the front room, where the light was stronger.

'That horrid case has got on my mind,' he thought; 'I shall be glad of a change of scene and air.' In the sitting-room, however, he was not pleased to hear again that stealthy tread upon the stairs, and to realize that it was much closer than before, as well as unmistakably real. And this time he got up and went out to see who it could be creeping about on the upper staircase at so late an hour.

But the sound ceased; there was no one visible on the stairs. He went to the floor below, not without trepidation, and turned on the electric light to make sure that no one was hiding in the empty rooms of the unoccupied suite. There was not a stick of furniture large enough to hide a dog. Then he called over the banisters to Mrs Monks, but there was no answer, and his voice echoed down into the dark vault of the house, and was lost in the roar of the gale that howled outside. Everyone was in bed and asleep—everyone except himself and the owner of this soft and stealthy tread.

'My absurd imagination, I suppose,' he thought. 'It must have been the wind after all, although—it seemed so *very* real and close, I thought.' He went back to his packing. It was by this time getting on towards midnight. He drank his coffee up and lit another pipe—the last before turning in.

It is difficult to say exactly at what point fear begins, when the causes of that fear are not plainly before the eyes. Impressions gather on the surface of the mind, film by film, as ice gathers upon the surface of still water, but often so lightly that they claim no definite recognition from the consciousness. Then a point is reached where the accumulated impressions become a definite emotion, and the mind realizes that something has happened. With something of a start, Johnson suddenly recognized that he felt nervous—oddly nervous; also, that for some time past the causes of this feeling had been gathering slowly in his mind, but that he had only just reached the point where he was forced to acknowledge them.

It was a singular and curious malaise that had come over him, and he hardly knew what to make of it. He felt as though he were doing something that was strongly objected to by another person, another person, moreover, who had some right to object. It was a most disturbing and disagreeable feeling, not unlike the persistent promptings of conscience: almost, in fact, as if he were doing something he knew to be wrong. Yet, though he searched vigorously and honestly in his mind, he could nowhere lay his finger upon the secret of this growing uneasiness, and it perplexed him. More, it distressed and frightened him.

'Pure nerves, I suppose,' he said aloud with a forced laugh.

'Mountain air will cure all that! Ah,' he added, still speaking to himself, 'and that reminds me—my snow-glasses.'

He was standing by the door of the bedroom during this brief soliloquy, and as he passed quickly towards the sitting-room to fetch them from the cupboard he saw out of the corner of his eye the indistinct outline of a figure standing on the stairs, a few feet from the top. It was someone in a stooping position, with one hand on the banisters, and the face peering up towards the landing. And at the same moment he heard a shuffling footstep. The person who had been creeping about below all this time had at last come up to his own floor. Who in the world could it be? And what in the name of Heaven did he want?

Johnson caught his breath sharply and stood stock still. Then, after a few seconds' hesitation, he found his courage, and turned to investigate. The stairs, he saw to his utter amazement, were empty; there was no one. He felt a series of cold shivers run over him, and something about the muscles of his legs gave a little and grew weak. For the space of several minutes he peered steadily into the shadows that congregated about the top of the staircase where he had seen the figure, and then he walked fast—almost ran, in fact—into the light of the front room; but hardly had he passed inside the doorway when he heard someone come up the stairs behind him with a quick bound and go swiftly into his bedroom. It was a heavy, but at the same time a stealthy footstep—the tread of somebody who did not wish to be seen. And it was at this precise moment that the nervousness he had hitherto experienced leaped the boundary line, and entered the state of fear, almost of acute, unreasoning fear. Before it turned into terror there was a further boundary to cross, and beyond that again lay the region of pure horror. Johnson's position was an unenviable one.

'By Jove! That *was* someone on the stairs, then,' he muttered, his flesh crawling all over; 'and whoever it was has now gone into my bedroom.' His delicate, pale face turned absolutely white, and for some minutes he hardly knew what to think or do. Then he realized intuitively that delay only set a premium upon fear; and he crossed the landing boldly and went straight into the other room, where, a few seconds before, the steps had disappeared.

'Who's there? Is that you, Mrs Monks?' he called aloud, as he went, and heard the first half of his words echo down the empty stairs, while the second half fell dead against the curtains in a room that apparently held no other human figure than his own.

'Who's there?' he called again, in a voice unnecessarily loud and that only just held firm. 'What do you want here?'

The curtains swayed very slightly, and, as he saw it, his heart felt as if it almost missed a beat; yet he dashed forward and drew them aside with a rush. A window, streaming with rain, was all that met his gaze. He continued his search, but in vain; the cupboards held nothing but rows of clothes, hanging motionless; and under the bed there was no sign of anyone hiding. He stepped backwards into the middle of the room, and, as he did so, something all but tripped him up. Turning with a sudden spring of alarm he saw—the kit-bag.

'Odd!' he thought. 'That's not where I left it!' A few moments before it had surely been on his right, between the bed and the bath; he did not remember having moved it. It was very curious. What in the world was the matter with everything? Were all his senses gone queer? A terrific gust of wind tore at the windows, dashing the sleet against the glass with the force of small gunshot, and then fled away howling dismally over the waste of Bloomsbury roofs. A sudden vision of the Channel next day rose in his mind and recalled him sharply to realities.

'There's no one here at any rate; that's quite clear!' he exclaimed aloud. Yet at the time he uttered them he knew perfectly well that his words were not true and that he did not believe them himself. He felt exactly as though someone was hiding close about him, watching all his movements, trying to hinder his packing in some way. 'And two of my senses,' he added, keeping up the pretence, 'have played me the most absurd tricks: the steps I heard and the figure I saw were both entirely imaginary.'

He went back to the front room, poked the fire into a blaze, and sat down before it to think. What impressed him more than anything else was the fact that the kit-bag was no longer where he had left it. It had been dragged nearer to the door.

What happened afterwards that night happened, of course, to a man already excited by fear, and was perceived by a mind that had not the full and proper control, therefore, of the senses. Outwardly, Johnson remained calm and master of himself to the end, pretending to the very last that everything witnessed had a natural explanation, or was merely delusions of his tired nerves. But inwardly, in his very heart, he knew all along that someone had been hiding downstairs in the empty suite when he came in, that this person had watched his opportunity and then stealthily made his way up to the bedroom, and that all he saw and heard afterwards, from the moving of the kit-bag to—well, to the other things this story has to tell—were caused directly by the presence of this invisible person.

And it was here, just when he most desired to keep his mind and thoughts controlled, that the vivid pictures received day after day upon the mental plates exposed in the courtroom of the Old Bailey, came strongly to light and developed themselves in the dark room of his inner vision. Unpleasant, haunting memories have a way of coming to life again just when the mind least desires them—in the silent watches of the night, on sleepless pillows, during the lonely hours spent by sick and dying beds. And so now, in the same way, Johnson saw nothing but the dreadful face of John Turk, the murderer, lowering at him from every corner of his mental field of vision; the white skin, the evil eyes, and the fringe of black hair low over the forehead. All the pictures of those ten days in court crowded back into his mind unbidden, and very vivid.

'This is all rubbish and nerves,' he exclaimed at length, springing with sudden energy from his chair. 'I shall finish my packing and go to bed. I'm overwrought, overtired. No doubt, at this rate I shall hear steps and things all night!'

But his face was deadly white all the same. He snatched up his field-glasses and walked across to the bedroom, humming a music-hall song as he went—a trifle too loud to be natural; and the instant he crossed the threshold and stood within the room something turned cold about his heart, and he felt that every hair on his head stood up.

The kit-bag lay close in front of him, several feet nearer to the door than he had left it, and just over its crumpled top he saw a head and face slowly sinking down out of sight as though someone were crouching behind it to hide, and at the same moment a sound like a long-drawn sigh was distinctly audible in the still air about him between the gusts of the storm outside.

Johnson had more courage and will-power than the girlish indecision on his face indicated; but at first such a wave of terror came over him that for some seconds he could do nothing but stand and stare. A violent trembling ran down his back and legs, and he was conscious of a foolish, almost a hysterical, impulse to scream aloud. That sigh seemed in his very ear, and the air still quivered with it. It was unmistakably a human sigh.

'Who's there?' he said at length, finding his voice; but though he meant to speak with loud decision, the tones came out instead in a faint whisper, for he had partly lost the control of his tongue and lips.

He stepped forward, so that he could see all round and over

the kit-bag. Of course there was nothing there, nothing but the faded carpet and the bulging canvas sides. He put out his hands and threw open the mouth of the sack where it had fallen over, being only three parts full, and then he saw for the first time that round the inside, some six inches from the top, there ran a broad smear of dull crimson. It was an old and faded blood stain. He uttered a scream, and drew back his hands as if they had been burnt. At the same moment the kit-bag gave a faint, but unmistakable, lurch forward towards the door.

Johnson collapsed backwards, searching with his hands for the support of something solid, and the door, being further behind him than he realized, received his weight just in time to prevent his falling, and shut to with a resounding bang. At the same moment the swinging of his left arm accidentally touched the electric switch, and the light in the room went out.

It was an awkward and disagreeable predicament, and if Johnson had not been possessed of real pluck he might have done all manner of foolish things. As it was, however, he pulled himself together, and groped furiously for the little brass knob to turn the light on again. But the rapid closing of the door had set the coats hanging on it a-swinging, and his fingers became entangled in a confusion of sleeves and pockets, so that it was some moments before he found the switch. And in those few moments of bewilderment and terror two things happened that sent him beyond recall over the boundary into the region of genuine horror—he distinctly heard the kit-bag shuffling heavily across the floor in jerks, and close in front of his face sounded once again the sigh of a human being.

In his anguished efforts to find the brass button on the wall he nearly scraped the nails from his fingers, but even then, in those frenzied moments of alarm—so swift and alert are the impressions of a mind keyed-up by a vivid emotion—he had time to realize that he dreaded the return of the light, and that it might be better for him to stay hidden in the merciful screen of darkness. It was but the impulse of a moment, however, and before he had time to act upon it he had yielded automatically to the original desire, and the room was flooded again with light.

But the second instinct had been right. It would have been better for him to have stayed in the shelter of the darkness. For there, close before him, bending over the half-packed kit-bag, clear as life in the merciless glare of the electric light, stood the figure of John Turk, the murderer. Not three feet from him the man stood, the fringe of black hair marked plainly against the pallor of the forehead, the whole horrible resentment of the scoundrel, as vivid as he had seen him day after day in the Old Bailey, when he stood there in the dock, cynical and callous, under the very shadow of the gallows.

In a flash Johnson realized what it all meant: the dirty and much-used bag; the smear of crimson within the top; the dreadful stretched condition of the bulging sides. He remembered how the victim's body had been stuffed into a canvas bag for burial, the ghastly, dismembered fragments forced with lime into this very bag; and the bag itself produced as evidence—it all came back to him as clear as day . . .

Very softly and stealthily his hand groped behind him for the handle of the door, but before he could actually turn it the very thing that he most of all dreaded came about, and John Turk lifted his devil's face and looked at him. At the same moment that heavy sigh passed through the air of the room, formulated somehow into words: 'It's my bag. And I want it.'

Johnson just remembered clawing the door open, and then falling in a heap upon the floor of the landing, as he tried frantically to make his way into the front room.

He remained unconscious for a long time, and it was still dark when he opened his eyes and realized that he was lying, stiff and bruised, on the cold boards. Then the memory of what he had seen rushed back into his mind, and he promptly fainted again. When he woke the second time the wintry dawn was just beginning to peep in at the windows, painting the stairs a cheerless, dismal grey, and he managed to crawl into the front room, and cover himself with an overcoat in the armchair, where at length he fell asleep.

A great clamour woke him. He recognized Mrs Monks's voice, loud and voluble.

'What! You ain't been to bed, sir! Are you ill, or has something 'appened? And there's an urgent gentleman to see you, though it ain't seven o'clock yet, and ——'

'Who is it?' he stammered. 'I'm all right, thanks. Fell asleep in my chair, I suppose.'

'Someone from Mr Wilb'rim's, and he says he ought to see you quick before you go abroad, and I told him ——'

'Show him up, please, at once,' said Johnson, whose head was whirling, and his mind was still full of dreadful visions.

Mr Wilbraham's man came in with many apologies, and explained briefly and quickly that an absurd mistake had been made, and that the wrong kit-bag had been sent over the night before.

'Henry somehow got hold of the one that came over from the courtroom, and Mr Wilbraham only discovered it when he saw his own lying in his room, and asked why it had not gone to you,' the man said.

'Oh!' said Johnson stupidly.

'And he must have brought you the one from the murder case instead, sir, I'm afraid,' the man continued, without the ghost of an expression on his face. 'The one John Turk packed the dead body in. Mr Wilbraham's awful upset about it, sir, and told me to come over first thing this morning with the right one, as you were leaving by the boat.'

He pointed to a clean-looking kit-bag on the floor, which he had just brought. 'And I was to bring the other one back, sir,' he added casually.

For some minutes Johnson could not find his voice. At last he pointed in the direction of his bedroom. 'Perhaps you would kindly unpack it for me. Just empty the things out on the floor.'

The man disappeared into the other room, and was gone for five minutes. Johnson heard the shifting to and fro of the bag, and the rattle of the skates and boots being unpacked.

'Thank you, sir,' the man said, returning with the bag folded over his arm. 'And can I do anything more to help you, sir?'

'What is it?' asked Johnson, seeing that he still had something he wished to say.

The man shuffled and looked mysterious. 'Beg pardon, sir, but knowing your interest in the Turk case, I thought you'd maybe like to know what's happened ——'

'Yes.'

'John Turk killed hisself last night with poison immediately on getting his release, and he left a note for Mr Wilbraham saying as he'd be much obliged if they'd have him put away, same as the woman he murdered, in the old kit-bag.'

'What time—did he do it?' asked Johnson.

'Ten o'clock last night, sir, the warder says.'

THE FACTS IN THE CASE OF M. VALDEMAR

Edgar Allen Poe

Of course I shall not pretend to consider it any matter for wonder, that the extraordinary case of M. Valdemar has excited discussion. It would have been a miracle had it not—especially under the circumstances. Through the desire of all parties concerned, to keep the affair from the public, at least for the present, or until we had further opportunities for investigation—through our endeavors to effect this—a garbled or exaggerated account made its way into society, and became the source of many unpleasant misrepresentations; and, very naturally, of a great deal of disbelief.

It is now rendered necessary that I give the *facts*—as far as I comprehend them myself. They are, succinctly, these:

My attention, for the last three years, had been repeatedly drawn to the subject of Mesmerism; and, about nine months ago, it occurred to me, quite suddenly, that in the series of experiments made hitherto, there had been a very remarkable and most unaccountable omission:—no person had as yet been mesmerized *in articulo mortis*. It remained to be seen, first, whether, in such condition, there existed in the patient any susceptibility to the magnetic influence; secondly, whether, if any existed, it was impaired or increased by the condition; thirdly, to what extend, or for how long a period, the encroachments of Death might be arrested by the process. There were other points to be ascertained, but these most excited my curiosity—the last in especial, from the immensely important character of its consequences.

In looking around me for some subject by whose means I might test these particulars, I was brought to think of my friend, M. Ernest Valdemar, the well-known compiler of "Bibliotheca Forensica," and author (under the *nom de plume* of Issachar Marx) of the Polish versions of "Wallenstein" and "Gargantua." M. Valdemar, who has resided principally at Harlem, N.Y., since the year 1839, is (or was) particularly noticeable for the extreme spareness of his person—his lower limbs much resembling those of John Randolph; and, also, for the whiteness of his whiskers, in violent contrast to the blackness of his hair—the latter, in consequence, being very generally mistaken for a wig. His temperament was markedly nervous, and rendered him a good subject for mesmeric experiment. On two or three occasions I had put him to sleep with little difficulty, but was disappointed in other results which his peculiar constitution had naturally led me to anticipate. His will was at no period positively, or thoroughly, under my control, and in regard to *clairvoyance*, I could accomplish with him nothing to be relied upon. I always attributed my failure at these points to the disordered state of his health. For some months previous to my becoming acquainted with him, his physicians had declared him in a confirmed phthisis. It was his custom, indeed, to speak calmly of his approaching dissolution, as of a matter neither to be avoided nor regretted.

When the ideas to which I have alluded first occurred to me, it was of course very natural that I should think of M. Valdemar. I knew the steady philosophy of the man too well to apprehend any scruples from *him;* and he had no relatives in America who would be likely to interfere. I spoke to him frankly upon the subject; and, to my surprise, his interest seemed vividly excited. I say to my surprise, for, although he had always yielded his person freely to my experiments, he had never before given me any tokens of sympathy with what I did. His disease was of that character which would admit of exact calculation in respect to the epoch of its termination in death; and it was finally arranged between us that he would send for me about twenty-four hours before the period announced by his physicians as that of his decease.

It is now rather more than seven months since I received, from M. Valdemar himself, the subjoined note:

"My Dear P——,
"You may as well come *now.* D—— and F—— are agreed that I cannot hold out beyond to-morrow midnight; and I think they have hit the time very nearly.

Valdemar."

I received this note within half an hour after it was written, and in fifteen minutes more I was in the dying man's chamber. I had not seen him for ten days, and was appalled by the fearful alteration which the brief interval had wrought in him. His face wore a leaden hue; the eyes were utterly lustreless; and the emaciation was so extreme, that the skin had been broken through by the cheek-bones. His expectoration was excessive. The pulse was barely perceptible. He retained, nevertheless, in a very remarkable manner, both his mental power and a certain degree of physical strength. He spoke with distinctness—took some palliative medicines without aid—and, when I entered the room, was occupied in penciling memoranda in a pocket-book. He was propped up in the bed by pillows. Doctors D—— and F—— were in attendance.

After pressing Valdemar's hand, I took these gentlemen aside, and obtained from them a minute account of the patient's condition. The left lung had been for eighteen months in a semi-osseous or cartilaginous state, and was, of course, entirely useless for all purposes of vitality. The right, in its upper portion, was also partially, if not thoroughly, ossified, while the lower region was merely a mass of purulent tubercles, running one into another. Several extensive perforations existed; and, at one point, permanent adhesion to the ribs had taken place. These appearances in the right lobe were of comparatively recent date. The ossification had proceeded with very unusual rapidity; no sign of it had been discovered a month before, and the adhesion had only been observed during the three previous days. Independently of the phthisis, the patient was suspected of aneurism of the aorta; but on this point the osseous symptoms rendered an exact diagnosis impossible. It was the opinion of both physicians that M. Valdemar would die about midnight on the morrow (Sunday). It was then seven o'clock on Saturday evening.

On quitting the invalid's bed-side to hold conversation with myself, Doctors D—— and F—— had bidden him a final farewell. It had not been their intention to return; but, at my request, they agreed to look in upon the patient about ten the next night.

When they had gone, I spoke freely with M. Valdemar on the subject of his approaching dissolution, as well as, more particularly, of the experiment proposed. He still professed himself quite willing and even anxious to have it made, and urged me to commence it at once. A male and a female nurse were in attendance; but I did not feel myself altogether at liberty to engage in a task of this character with no more reliable witnesses than these people, in case of sudden accident, might prove. I therefore postponed operations until about eight the next night, when the arrival of a medical student with whom I had some acquaintance (Mr.

Theodore L——l), relieved me from father embarrassment. It had been my design, originally, to wait for the physicians, but I was induced to proceed, first, by the urgent entreaties of M. Valdemar, and secondly, by my conviction that I had not a moment to lose, as he was evidently sinking fast.

Mr. L——l was so kind as to accede to my desire that he would take notes of all that occurred; and it is from his memoranda that what I now have to relate is, for the most part, either condensed or copied *verbatim.*

It wanted about five minutes of eight when, taking the patient's hand, I begged him to state, as distinctly as he could, to Mr. L——l, whether he (M. Valdemar) was entirely willing that I should make the experiment of mesmerizing him in his then condition.

He replied feebly, yet quite audibly: "Yes, I wish to be mesmerized"—adding immediately afterward: "I fear you have deferred it too long."

While he spoke thus, I commenced the passes which I had already found most effectual in subduing him. He was evidently influenced with the first lateral stroke of my hand across his forehead; but, although I exerted all my powers, no farther perceptible effect was induced until some minutes after ten o'clock, when Doctors D—— and F—— called, according to appointment. I explained to them, in a few words, what I designed, and as they opposed no objection, saying that the patient was already in the death agony, I proceeded without hesitation—exchanging, however, the lateral passes for downward ones, and directing my gaze entirely into the right eye of the sufferer.

By this time his pulse was imperceptible and his breathing was stertorous, and at intervals of half a minute.

This condition was nearly unaltered for a quarter of an hour. At the expiration of this period, however, a natural although a very deep sigh escaped the bosom of the dying man, and the stertorous breathing ceased—that is to say, its stertorousness was no longer apparent; the intervals were undiminished. The patient's extremities were of an icy coldness.

At five minutes before eleven, I perceived unequivocal signs of the mesmeric influence. The glassy roll of the eye was changed for that expression of easy *inward* examination which is never seen except in cases of sleep-waking, and which it is quite impossible to mistake. With a few rapid lateral passes I made the lids quiver, as in incipient sleep, and with a few more I closed them altogether. I was not satisfied, however, with this, but continued the manipulations vigorously, and with the fullest exertion of the will, until I had completely stiffened the limbs of the slumberer, after placing them in a seemingly easy position. The legs were at full length; the arms were nearly so, and reposed on the bed at a moderate distance from the loins. The head was very slightly elevated.

When I had accomplished this, it was fully midnight, and I requested the gentlemen present to examine M. Valdemar's condition. After a few experiments, they admitted him to be in an unusually perfect state of mesmeric trance. The curiosity of both the physicians was greatly excited. Dr. D—— resolved at once to remain with the patient all night, while Dr. F—— took leave with a promise to return to daybreak. Mr. L——l and the nurses remained.

We left M. Valdemar entirely undisturbed until about three o'clock in the morning, when I approached him and found him in precisely the same condition as when Dr. F—— went away—that is to say, he lay in the same position; the pulse was imperceptible; the breathing was gentle (scarcely noticeable, unless through the application of a mirror to the lips); the eyes were closed naturally; and the limbs were as rigid and cold as marble. Still, the general appearance was certainly not that of death.

As I approached M. Valdemar I made a kind of half effort to

influence his right arm into pursuit of my own, as I passed the latter gently to and fro above his person. In such experiments with this patient, I had never perfectly succeeded before, and assuredly I had little thought of succeeding now; but to my astonishment, his arm very readily, although feebly, followed every direction I assigned it with mine. I determined to hazard a few words of conversation.

"M. Valdemar," I said, "are you asleep?" He made no answer, but I perceived a tremor about the lips, and was thus induced to repeat the question, again and again. At its third repetition, his whole frame was agitated by a very slight quivering; the eyelids unclosed themselves so far as to display a white line of a ball; the lips moved sluggishly, and from between them, in a barely audible whisper, issued the words:

"Yes—asleep now. Do not wake me!—let me die so!"

I here felt the limbs, and found them as rigid as ever. The right arm, as before, obeyed the direction of my hand. I questioned the sleep-waker again:

"Do you still feel pain in the breast, M. Valdemar?"

The answer now was immediate, but even less audible than before:

"No pain—I am dying!"

I did not think it advisable to disturb him farther just then, and nothing more was said or done until the arrival of Dr. F——, who came a little before sunrise, and expressed unbounded astonishment at finding the patient still alive. After feeling the pulse and applying a mirror to the lips, he requested me to speak to the sleep-waker again. I did so, saying:

"M. Valdemar, do you still sleep?"

As before, some minutes elapsed ere a reply was made; and during the interval the dying man seemed to be collecting his energies to speak. At my fourth repetition of the question, he said very faintly, almost inaudibly:

"Yes; still asleep—dying."

It was now the opinion, or rather the wish, of the physicians, that M. Valdemar should be suffered to remain undisturbed in his present apparently tranquil condition, until death should supervene—and this, it was generally agreed, must now take place within a few minutes. I concluded, however, to speak to him once more, and merely repeated my previous question.

While I spoke, there came a marked change over the countenance of the sleep-waker. The eyes rolled themselves slowly open, the pupils disappearing upwardly; the skin generally assumed a cadaverous hue, resembling not so much parchment as white paper; and the circular hectic spots which, hitherto, had been strongly defined in the centre of each cheek, *went out* at once. I use this expression, because the suddenness of their departure put me in mind of nothing so much as the extinguishment of a candle by a puff of the breath. The upper lip, at the same time, writhed itself away from the teeth, which it had previously covered completely; while the lower jaw fell with an audible jerk, leaving the mouth widely extended, and disclosing in full view the swollen and blackened tongue. I presume that no member of the party then present had been unaccustomed to death-bed horrors; but so hideous beyond conception was the appearance of M. Valdemar at this moment, that there was a general shrinking back from the region of the bed.

I now feel that I have reached a point of this narrative at which every reader will be startled into positive disbelief. It is my business, however, simply to proceed.

There was no longer the faintest sign of vitality in M. Valdemar; and concluding him to be dead, we were consigning him to the charge of the nurses, when a strong vibratory motion was observable in the tongue. This continued for perhaps a minute. At the expiration of this period, there issued from the distended and motionless jaws a voice—such as it would be madness in me to attempt describing. There are, indeed, two or three epithets which might be considered as applicable to it in part; I might say, for example, that the sound was harsh, and broken and hollow; but the hideous whole is indescribable, for the simple reason that no similar sounds have ever jarred upon the ear of humanity. There were two particulars, nevertheless, which I thought then, and still think, might fairly be stated as characteristic of the intonation—as well adapted to convey some idea of its unearthly peculiarity. In the first place, the voice seemed to reach our ears—at least mine—from a vast distance, or from some deep cavern within the earth. In the second place, it impressed me (I fear, indeed, that it will be impossible to make myself comprehended) as gelatinous or glutinous matters impress the sense of touch.

I have spoken both of "sound" and of "voice." I mean to say that the sound was one of distinct—of even wonderfully, thrillingly distinct—syllabification. M. Valdemar *spoke*—obviously in reply to the question I had propounded to him a few minutes before. I had asked him, it will be remembered, if he still slept. He now said:

"Yes!—no;—I *have* been sleeping—and now—now—*I am dead.*"

No person present even affected to deny, or attempted to repress, the unutterable, shuddering horror which these few words, thus uttered, were so well calculated to convey. Mr. L——l (the student) swooned. The nurses immediately left the chamber, and could not be induced to return. My own impressions I would not pretend to render intelligible to the reader. For nearly an hour, we busied ourselves, silently—without the utterance of a word—in endeavors to revive L——l. When he came to himself, we addressed ourselves again to an investigation of M. Valdemar's condition.

It remained in all respects as I have last described it, with the exception that the mirror no longer afforded evidence of respiration. An attempt to draw blood from the arm failed. I should mention, too, that this limb was no further subject to my will. I endeavored in vain to make it follow the direction of my hand. The only real indication, indeed, of the mesmeric influence, was now found in the vibratory movement of the tongue, whenever I addressed M. Valdemar a question. He seemed to be making an effort to reply, but had no longer sufficient volition. To queries put to him by any other person than myself he seemed utterly insensible—although I endeavored to place each member of the company in mesmeric *rapport* with him. I believe that I have now related all that is necessary to an understanding of the sleep-waker's state at this epoch. Other nurses were procured; and at ten o'clock I left the house in company with the two physicians and Mr. L——l.

In the afternoon we all called again to see the patient. His condition remained precisely the same. We had now some discussion as to the propriety and feasibility of awakening him; but we had little difficulty in agreeing that no good purpose would be served by so doing. It was evident that, so far, death (or what is usually termed death) had been arrested by the mesmeric process. It seemed clear to us all that to awaken M. Valdemar would be merely to insure his instant, or at least his speedy, dissolution.

From this period until the close of last week—*an interval of nearly seven months*—we continued to make daily calls at M. Valdemar's house, accompanied, now and then, by medical and other friends. All this time the sleep-waker remained *exactly* as I have last described him. The nurses' attentions were continual.

It was on Friday last that we finally resolved to make the experiment of awakening, or attempting to awaken him, and it is the (perhaps) unfortunate result of this latter experiment which has given rise to so much discussion in private circles—to so much of what I cannot help thinking unwarranted popular feeling.

For the purpose of relieving M. Valdemar from the mesmeric trance, I made use of the customary passes. These for a time were unsuccessful. The first indication of revival was afforded by a partial descent of the iris. It was observed, as especially remarkable, that this lowering of the pupil was accompanied by the profuse outflowing of a yellowish ichor (from beneath the lids) of a pungent and highly offensive odor.

It was now suggested that I should attempt to influence the patient's arm as heretofore. I made the attempt and failed. Dr. F—— then intimated a desire to have me put a question. I did so, as follows:

"M. Valdemar, can you explain to us what are your feelings or wishes now?"

There was an instant return of the hectic circles on the cheeks: the tongue quivered, or rather rolled violently in the mouth (although the jaws and lips remained rigid as before), and at length the same hideous voice which I have already described, broke forth:

"For God's sake—quick!—quick!—put me to sleep—or, quick!—waken me!—quick!—*I say to you that I am dead!*"

I was thoroughly unnerved, and for an instant remained undecided what to do. At first I made an endeavor to recompose the patient; but, failing in this through total abeyance of the will, I retracted my steps and as earnestly struggled to awaken him. In this attempt I soon saw that I should be successful—or at least I soon fancied that my success would be complete—and I am sure that all in the room were prepared to see the patient awaken.

For what really occurred, however, it is quite impossible that any human being could have been prepared.

As I rapidly made the mesmeric passes, amid ejaculations of "dead! dead!" absolutely *bursting* from the tongue and not from the lips of the sufferer, his whole frame at once—within the space of a single minute, or even less, shrunk—crumbled, absolutely *rotted* away beneath my hands. Upon the bed, before the whole company, there lay a nearly liquid mass of loathsome—of detestable putridity.

SMEE

A. M. Burrage

'**N**o,' said Jackson, with a deprecatory smile, 'I'm sorry. I don't want to upset your game. I shan't be doing that because you'll have plenty without me. But I'm not playing any games of hide-and-seek.'

It was Christmas Eve, and we were a party of fourteen with just the proper leavening of youth. We had dined well; it was the season for childish games, and we were all in the mood for playing them—all, that is, except Jackson. When somebody suggested hide-and-seek there was rapturous and almost unanimous approval. His was the one dissentient voice.

It was not like Jackson to spoil sport or refuse to do as others wanted. Somebody asked him if he were feeling seedy.

'No,' he answered, 'I feel perfectly fit, thanks. But,' he added with a smile softened without retracting the flat refusal, 'I'm not playing hide-and-seek.'

One of us asked him why not. He hesitated for some seconds before replying.

'I sometimes go and stay at a house where a girl was killed through playing hide-and-seek in the dark. She didn't know the house very well. There was a servants' staircase with a door to it. When she was pursued she opened the door and jumped into what she must have thought was one of the bedrooms—and she broke her neck at the bottom of the stairs.

We all looked concerned, and Mrs Fernley said:

'How awful! And you were there when it happened?'

Jackson shook his head very gravely. 'No,' he said, 'but I was there when something else happened. Something worse.'

'I shouldn't have thought anything could be worse.'

'This was,' said Jackson, and shuddered visibly. 'Or so it seemed to me.'

I think he wanted to tell the story and was angling for encouragement. A few requests which may have seemed to him to lack urgency, he affected to ignore and went off at a tangent.

'I wonder if any of you have played a game called "Smee." It's a great improvement on the ordinary game of hide-and-seek. The name derives from the ungrammatical colloquialism, "It's me." You might care to play if you're going to play a game of that sort. Let me tell you the rules.

'Every player is presented with a sheet of paper. All the sheets are blank except one, on which is written "Smee." Nobody knows who is "Smee" except "Smee" himself—or herself, as the case may be. The lights are then turned out and "Smee" slips from the room and goes off to hide, and after an interval the other players go off in search, without knowing whom they are actually in search of. One player meeting another challenges with the word "Smee" and the other player, if not the one concerned, answers "Smee."

'The real "Smee" makes no answer when challenged, and the second player remains quietly by him. Presently they will be discovered by a third player, who, having challenged and received no answer, will link up with the first two. This goes on until all the players have formed a chain, and the last to join is marked down for a forfeit. It's a good noisy, romping game, and in a big house it often takes a long time to complete the chain. You might care to try it; and I'll pay my forfeit and smoke one of Tim's excellent cigars here by the fire until you get tired of it.'

I remarked that it sounded a good game and asked Jackson if he had played it himself.

'Yes,' he answered; 'I played it in the house I was telling you about.'

'And *she* was there? The girl who broke—'

'No, no,' Mrs Fernley interrupted. 'He told us he wasn't there when it happened.'

Jackson considered. 'I don't know if she was there or not. I'm afraid she was. I know that there were thirteen of us and there ought only to have been twelve. And I'll swear that I didn't know her name, or I think I should have gone clean off my head when I heard that whisper in the dark. No, you don't catch me playing that game, or any other like it, any more. It spoiled my nerve quite a while, and I can't afford to take long holidays. Besides, it saves a lot of trouble and inconvenience to own up at once to being a coward.'

Tim Vouce, the best of hosts, smiled around at us, and in that smile there was a meaning which is sometimes vulgarly expressed by the slow closing of an eye. 'There's a story coming,' he announced.

'There's certainly a story of sorts,' said Jackson, 'but whether it's coming or not—' He paused and shrugged his shoulders.

'Well, you're going to pay a forfeit instead of playing?'

'Please. But have a heart and let me down lightly. It's not just a sheer cussedness on my part.'

'Payment in advance,' said Tim, 'insures honesty and promotes good feeling. You are therefore sentenced to tell the story here and now.'

And here follows Jackson's story, unrevised by me and passed on without comment to a wider public:

Some of you, I know, have run across the Sangstons. Christopher Sangston and his wife, I mean. They're distant connections of mine—at least, Violet Sangston is. About eight years ago they bought a house between the North and South Downs on the Surrey and Sussex border, and five years ago they invited me to come and spend Christmas with them.

It was a fairly old house—I couldn't say exactly of what period—and it certainly deserved the epithet 'rambling.' It wasn't a particularly big house, but the original architect, whoever he may have been, had not concerned himself with economising in space, and at first you could get lost in it quite easily.

Well, I went down for that Christmas, assured by Violet's letter that I knew most of my fellow-guests and that the two or three who might be strangers to me were all 'lambs.' Unfortunately, I'm one of the world's workers, and I couldn't get away until Christmas Eve, although the other members of the party had assembled on the preceding day. Even then I had to cut it rather fine to be there for dinner on my first night. They were all dressing when I arrived and I had to go straight to my room and waste no time. I may even have kept dinner waiting a bit, for I was last down, and it was announced within a minute of my entering the drawing-room. There was just time to say 'hullo' to everybody I knew, to be briefly introduced to the two or three I didn't know, and then I had to give my arm to Mrs Gorman.

I mention this as the reason why I didn't catch the name of a tall, dark, handsome girl I hadn't met before. Everything was rather hurried and I am always bad at catching people's names. She looked cold and clever and rather forbidding, the sort of girl who gives the impression of knowing all about men and the more she knows of them the less she likes them. I felt that I wasn't going to hit it off with this particular 'lamb' of Violet's, but she looked interesting all the same, and I wondered who she was. I didn't ask, because I was pretty sure of hearing somebody address her by name before very long.

Unluckily, though, I was a long way off her at table, and as Mrs Gorman was at the top of her form that night I soon forgot to worry about who she might be. Mrs Gorman is one of the most amusing women I know, an outrageous but quite innocent flirt, with a very sprightly wit which isn't always unkind. She can think half a dozen moves ahead in conversation just as an expert can in a game of chess. We were soon sparring, or, rather, I was 'covering' against the ropes, and I quite forgot to ask her in an undertone the name of the cold, proud beauty. The lady on the other side of me was a stranger, or had been until a few minutes since, and I didn't think of seeking information in that quarter.

There was a round dozen of us, including the Sangstons themselves, and we were all young or trying to be. The Sangstons themselves were the oldest members of the party and their son Reggie, in his last year at Marlborough, must have been the youngest. When there was talk of playing games after dinner it was he who suggested 'Smee.' He told us how to play it just as I've described it to you.

His father chipped in as soon as we all understood what was going to be required of us. 'If there are any games of that sort going on in the house,' he said, 'for goodness' sake be careful of the back stairs on the first-floor landing. There's a door to them and I've often meant to take it down. In the dark anybody who doesn't know the house very well might think they were walking into a room. A girl actually did break her neck on those stairs about ten years ago when the Ainsties lived here.'

I asked how it happened.

'Oh,' said Sangston, 'there was a party here one Christmas time and they were playing hide-and-seek as you propose doing. This girl was one of the hiders. She heard somebody coming, ran along the passage to get away, and opened the door of what she thought was a bedroom, evidently with the intention of hiding behind it while her pursuer went past. Unfortunately it was the door leading to the back stairs, and that staircase is as straight and almost as steep as the shaft of a pit. She was dead when they picked her up.'

We all promised for our own sakes to be careful. Mrs Gorman said that she was sure nothing could happen to her, since she was insured by three different firms, and her next-of-kin was a brother whose consistent ill-luck was a byword in the family. You see, none of us had known the unfortunate girl, and as the tragedy was ten years old there was no need to pull long faces about it.

Well, we started the game almost immediately after dinner. The men allowed themselves only five minutes before joining the ladies, and then young Reggie Sangston went round and assured himself that the lights were out all over the house except in the servants' quarters and in the drawing-room where we were assembled. We then got busy with twelve sheets of paper which he twisted into pellets and shook up between his hands before passing them round. Eleven of them were blank, and 'Smee' was written on the twelfth. The person drawing the latter was the one who had to hide. I looked and saw that mine was a blank. A moment later out went the electric lights, and in the darkness I heard somebody get up and creep to the door.

After a minute or so somebody gave a signal and we made a rush for the door. I for one hadn't the least idea which of the party was 'Smee'. For five or ten minutes we were all rushing up and down passages and in and out rooms challenging one another and answering, '*Smee?—Smee!*'

After a bit the alarums and excursions died down, and I guessed that 'Smee' was found. Eventually I found a chain of people all sitting still and holding their breath on some narrow stairs leading up to a row of attics. I hastily joined it, having challenged and been answered with silence, and presently two more stragglers arrived, each racing the other to avoid being last. Sangston was one of them, indeed it was he who was marked down for a forfeit, and after a little while he remarked in an undertone, 'I think we're all here now, aren't we?'

He struck a match, looked up the shaft of the staircase, and began to count. It wasn't hard, although we just about filled the staircase, for we were sitting each a step or two above the next, and all our heads were visible.

'. . . nine, ten, eleven, twelve—*thirteen*,' he concluded, and then laughed. 'Dash it all, that's one too many!'

The match had burned out and he struck another and began to count. He got as far as twelve, and then uttered an exclamation.

'There are thirteen people here!' he exclaimed. 'I haven't counted myself yet.'

'Oh, nonsense!' I laughed. 'You probably began with yourself, and now you want to count yourself twice.'

Out came his son's electric torch, giving a brighter and steadier light and we all began to count. Of course we numbered twelve.

Sangston laughed.

'Well,' he said, 'I could have sworn I counted thirteen twice.'

From halfway up the stairs came Violet Sangston's voice with a little nervous trill in it. 'I thought there was somebody sitting two steps above me. Have you moved up, Captain Ransome?'

Ransome said that he hadn't: he also said that he thought there was somebody sitting between Violet and himself. Just for a moment there was an uncomfortable Something in the air, a little cold ripple which touched us all. For that little moment it seemed to all of us, I think, that something odd and unpleasant had happened and was liable to happen again. Then we laughed at ourselves and at one another and were comfortable once more. There *were* only twelve of us, and there *could* only have been twelve of us, and there was no argument about it. Still laughing we trooped back to the drawing-room to begin again.

This time I was 'Smee,' and Violet Sangston ran me to earth while I was still looking for a hiding-place. That round didn't last long, and we were a chain of twelve within two or three minutes. Afterwards there was a short interval. Violet wanted a wrap fetched for her, and her husband went up to get it from her room. He was no sooner gone than Reggie pulled me by the sleeve. I saw that he was looking pale and sick.

'Quick!' he whispered, 'while father's out of the way. Take me into the smoke room and give me a brandy or a whisky or something.'

Outside the room I asked him what was the matter, but he didn't answer at first, and I thought it better to dose him first and question him afterward. So I mixed him a pretty dark-complexion brandy and soda which he drank at a gulp and then began to puff as if he had been running.

'I've had rather a turn,' he said to me with a sheepish grin.

'What's the matter?'

'I don't know. You were "Smee" just now, weren't you? Well, of course I didn't know who "Smee" was, and while mother and the others ran into the west wing and found you, I turned east. There's a deep clothes cupboard in my bedroom—I'd marked it down as a good place to hide when it was my turn, and I had an idea that "Smee" might be there. I opened the door in the dark, felt round, and touched somebody's hand. "Smee?" I whispered, and not getting any answer I thought I had found "Smee."

"Well, I don't know how it was, but an odd creepy feeling came over me, I can't describe it, but I felt that something was wrong. So I turned on my electric torch and there was nobody there. Now, I swear I touched a hand, and I was filling up the doorway of the cupboard at the time, so nobody could get out and past me.' He puffed again. 'What do you make of it?' he asked.

'You imagined that you had touched a hand,' I answered, naturally enough.

He uttered a short laugh. 'Of course I knew you were going to say that,' he said. 'I must have imagined it, mustn't I?' He paused and swallowed. 'I mean, it couldn't have been anything else *but* imagination, could it?'

I assured him that it couldn't, meaning what I said, and he accepted this, but rather with the philosophy of one who knows he is right but doesn't expect to be believed. We returned together to the drawing-room where, by that time, they were all waiting for us and ready to start again.

It may have been my imagination—although I'm almost sure it wasn't—but it seemed to me that all enthusiasm for the game had suddenly melted like a white frost in strong sunlight. If anybody had suggested another game I'm sure we should all have been grateful and abandoned 'Smee.' Only nobody did. Nobody seemed to like to. I for one, and I can speak for some of the others too, was oppressed with the feeling that there was something wrong. I couldn't have said what I thought was wrong, indeed I didn't think about it at all, but somehow all the sparkle had gone out of the fun, and hovering over my mind like a shadow was the warning of some sixth sense which told me that there was an influence in the house which was neither sane, sound nor healthy. Why did I feel like that? Because Sangston had counted thirteen of us instead of twelve, and his son had thought he had touched somebody in an empty cupboard. No, there was more in it than just that. One would have laughed at such things in the ordinary way, and it was just that feeling of something being wrong which stopped me from laughing.

Well, we started again, and when we went in pursuit of the unknown 'Smee,' we were as noisy as ever, but it seemed to me that most of us were acting. Frankly, for no reason other than the one I've given you, we'd stopped enjoying the game. I had an instinct to hunt with the main pack, but after a few minutes, during which no 'Smee' had been found, my instinct to play winning games and be first if possible, set me searching on my own account. And on the first floor of the west wing following the wall which was actually the shell of the house, I blundered against a pair of human knees.

I put out my hand and touched a soft, heavy curtain. Then I knew where I was. There were tall, deeply-recessed windows with seats along the landing, and curtains over the recesses to the ground. Somebody was sitting in a corner of this window-seat behind the curtain. Aha, I had caught 'Smee'! So I drew the curtain aside, stepped in, and touched the bare arm of a woman.

It was a dark night outside, and moreover, the window was not only curtained but a blind hung down to where the bottom panes joined up with the frame. Between the curtain and the window it was as dark as the plague of Egypt. I could not have seen my hand held six inches before my face, much less the woman sitting in the corner.

'Smee?' I whispered.

I had no answer. 'Smee' when challenged does not answer. So I sat down beside her, first in the field, to await the others. Then, having settled myself I leaned over to her and whispered:

'Who is it? What's your name, "Smee"?'

And out of the darkness beside me the whisper came back: 'Brenda Ford.'

I didn't know the name, but because I didn't know it I guessed at once who she was. The tall, pale, dark girl was the only person in the house I didn't know by name. Ergo my companion was the tall, pale, dark girl. It seemed rather intriguing to be there with her, shut in between a heavy curtain and a window, and I rather wondered whether she was enjoying the game we were all playing. Somehow she hadn't seemed to me to be one of the romping sort. I muttered one or two commonplace questions to her and had no answer.

'Smee' is a game of silence. 'Smee' and the person or persons who have found 'Smee' are supposed to keep quiet to make it hard for the others. But there was nobody else about, and it occurred to me that she was playing the game a little too much to the letter. I spoke again and got no answer, and then I began to be annoyed. She was of that cold, 'superior' type which affects to despise men; she didn't like me; and she was sheltering behind the rules of a game for children to be discourteous. Well, if she didn't like sitting there with me, I certainly didn't want to be sitting there with her! I half turned from her and began to hope that we should both be discovered without much more delay.

Having discovered that I didn't like being there alone with her, it was queer how soon I found myself hating it, and that for a reason very different from the one which had at first whetted my annoyance. The girl I had met for the first time before dinner, and seen diagonally across the table, had a sort of cold charm about her which had attracted while it had half angered me. For the girl who was with me, imprisoned in the opaque darkness between the curtain and the window, I felt no attraction at all. It was so very much the reverse that I should have wondered at myself if, after the first shock of the discovery that she had suddenly become repellent to me, I had had room in my mind for anything besides the consciousness that her close presence was an increasing horror to me.

It came upon me just as quickly as I've uttered the words. My flesh suddenly shrank from her as you see a strip of gelatin shrink and wither before the heat of a fire. That feeling of something being wrong had come back to me, but multiplied to an extent which turned foreboding into actual terror. I firmly believe that I should have got up and run if I had not felt that at my first movement she would have divined my intention and compelled me to stay, by some means of which I could not bear to think. The memory of having touched her bare arm made me wince and draw in my lips. I prayed that somebody else would come along soon.

My prayer was answered. Light footfalls sounded on the landing. Somebody on the other side of the curtain brushed again my knees. The curtain was drawn aside and a woman's hand, fumbling in the darkness, presently rested on my shoulder. 'Smee?' whispered a voice which I instantly recognised as Mrs Gorman's.

Of course she received no answer. She came and settled down beside me with a rustle, and I can't describe the sense of relief she brought me.

'It's Tony, isn't it?' she whispered.

'Yes,' I whispered back.

'You're not "Smee" are you?'

'No, she's on my other side.'

She reached a hand across me, and I heard one of her nails scratch the surface of a woman's silk gown.

'Hullo, "Smee"! How are you? *Who* are you? Oh, is it against the rules to talk? Never mind, Tony, we'll break the rules. Do you know, Tony, this game is beginning to irk me a little. I hope they're not going to run it to death by playing it all the evening. I'd like to play some game where we can all be together in the same room with a nice bright fire.'

'Same here,' I agreed fervently.

'Can't you suggest something when we go down? There's

something rather uncanny in this particular amusement. I can't quite shed the delusion that there's somebody in the game who oughtn't to be in at all.'

That was just how I had been feeling, but I didn't say so. But for my part the worst of my qualms were now gone; the arrival of Mrs Gorman had dissipated them. We sat on talking, wondering from time to time when the rest of the party would arrive.

I don't know how long elapsed before we heard a clatter of feet on the landing and young Reggie's voice shouting, 'Hullo! Hullo, there! Anybody there!'

'Yes,' I answered.

'Mrs Gorman with you?'

'Yes.'

'Well, you're a nice pair! You've both forfeited. We've all been waiting for you for hours.'

'Why, you haven't found "Smee" yet,' I objected.

'*You* haven't, you mean. I happen to have been "Smee" myself.'

'But "Smee's" here with us,' I cried.

'Yes,' agreed Mrs Gorman.

The curtain was stripped aside and in a moment we were blinking into the eye of Reggie's electric torch. I looked at Mrs Gorman and then on my other side. Between me and the wall there was an empty space on the window seat. I stoop up at once, and wished I hadn't, for I found myself sick and dizzy.

'There *was* somebody there,' I maintained, 'because I touched her.'

'So did I,' said Mrs Gorman in a voice which had lost its steadiness. 'And I don't see how she could have got up and gone without our knowing it.'

Reggie uttered a queer, shaken laugh. He, too, had had an unpleasant experience that evening. 'Somebody's been playing the goat,' he remarked. 'Coming down?'

We were not very popular when we arrived in the drawing-room. Reggie rather tactlessly gave it out that he had found us sitting on a window-seat behind the curtain. I taxed the tall, dark girl with having pretending to be 'Smee' and afterwards slipping away. She denied it. After which we settled down and played other games. 'Smee' was done with for the evening, and I for one was glad of it.

Some long while later, during an interval, Sangston told me, if I wanted a drink, to go into the smoke room and help myself. I went, and he presently followed me. I could see that he was rather peeved with me, and the reason came out during the following minute or two. It seemed, that, in his opinion, if I must sit out and flirt with Mrs Gorman—in circumstances which would have been considered highly compromising in his young days—I needn't do it during a round game and keep everybody waiting for us.

'But there was somebody else there,' I protested, 'somebody pretending to be "Smee." I believe it was that tall, dark girl, Miss Ford, although she denied it. She even whispered her name to me.'

Sangston stared at me and nearly dropped his glass.

'Miss *Who?*' he shouted.

'Brenda Ford—she told me her name was.'

Sangston put down his glass and laid a hand on my shoulder.

'Look here, old man,' he said, 'I don't mind a joke, but don't let it go too far. We don't want all the women in the house getting hysterical. Brenda Ford is the name of the girl who broke her neck on the stairs playing hide-and-seek here ten years ago.'

THE BISHOP'S GHOST AND THE PRINTER'S BABY

Frank R. Stockton

Around the walls of a certain old church there stood many tombs, and these had been there so long that the plaster with which their lids were fastened down had dried and crumbled, so that in most of them there were long cracks under their lids, and out of these the ghosts of the people who had been buried in the tombs were in the habit of escaping at night.

This had been going on for a long time, and, at the period of our story, the tombs were in such bad repair that every night the body of the church was so filled with ghosts that before daylight one of the sacristans were obliged to come into the church and sprinkle holy water everywhere. This was done to clear the church of ghosts before the first service began, and who does not know that if a ghost is sprinkled with holy water it shrivels up? This first service was attended almost exclusively by printers on their way home from their nightly labours on the journals of the town.

The tomb which had the largest crack under its lid belonged to a bishop who had died more than a hundred years before, and who had a great reputation for sanctity; so much so, indeed, that people had been in the habit of picking little pieces of plaster from under the lid of his tomb and carrying them away as holy relics to prevent diseases and accidents.

This tomb was more imposing than the others, and stood upon a pedestal, so that the crack beneath its lid was quite plain to view, and remarks had been made about having it repaired.

Very early one morning, before it was time for the first service, there came into the church a poor mason. His wife had recently recovered from a severe sickness, and he was desirous of making an offering to the church. But having no money to spare, he had determined that he would repair the bishop's tomb, and he consequently came to do this before his regular hours of work began.

All the ghosts were out of their tombs at the time, but they were gathered together in the other end of the church, and the mason did not see them, nor did they notice him; and he immediately went to work. He had brought some plaster and a trowel, and it was not long before the crack under the lid of the tomb was entirely filled up, and the plaster made as smooth and neat as when the tomb was new.

When his work was finished, the mason left the church by the little side door which had given him entrance.

Not ten minutes afterwards the sacristan came in to sprinkle the church with holy water. Instantly the ghosts began to scatter right and left, and to slip into their tombs as quickly as possible, but when the ghost of the good bishop reached his tomb, he found it impossible to get in. He went around and around it, but nowhere could he find the least little chink by which he could enter. The sacristan was walking along the other side of the church scattering holy water, and in great trepidation the bishop's ghost hastened from tomb to tomb, hoping to find one which was unoccupied into which he could slip before the sprinkling began on that side of the church. He soon came to one which he thought might be empty, but he discovered to his consternation that it was occupied by the ghost of a young girl who had died of love.

"Alas! alas!" exclaimed the bishop's ghost. "How unlucky! who would have supposed this to be your tomb?"

"It is not really my tomb," said the ghost of the young girl. "It is the tomb of Sir Geoffrey of the Marle, who was killed in battle nigh two centuries ago. I am told that it has been empty for a long time, for his ghost has gone to Castle Marle. Not long ago I came into the church, and, finding this tomb unoccupied I settled here."

"Ah, me!" said the bishop's ghost, "the sacristan will soon be round here with the holy water. Could not you get out and go to your own tomb; where is it?"

"Alas, good father," said the ghost of the young girl, "I have no tomb; I was buried plainly in the ground, and I do not know that I could find the place again. But I have no right to keep you out of this tomb, good father; it is as much yours as it is mine, so I will come out and let you enter; truly you are in great danger. As for me it does not matter very much whether I am sprinkled or not."

So the ghost of the young girl slipped out of Sir Geoffrey's tomb, and the bishop's ghost slipped in, but not a minute before the sacristan had reached the place. The ghost of the young girl flittered from one pillar to another until it came near to the door and there it paused, thinking what it should do next. Even if it could find the grave from which it had come, it did not want to go back to such a place; it liked churches better.

Soon the printers began to come in to the early morning service. One of them was very sad, and there were tears in his eyes.

He was a young man, not long married, and his child, a baby girl, was so sick that he scarcely expected to find it alive when he should reach home that morning.

The ghost of the young girl was attracted by the sorrowful printer, and when the service was over and he had left the church it followed him, keeping itself unseen. The printer found his wife in tears; the poor little baby was very low. It lay upon the bed, its eyes shut, its face pale and pinched, gasping for breath.

The mother was obliged to leave the room for a few moments to attend to some household affair, and her husband followed to comfort her, and when they were gone, the ghost of the young girl approached the bed and looked down on the little baby. It was nearer death than its parents supposed, and scarcely had they gone before it drew its last breath.

The ghost of the young girl bowed its head; it was filled with pity and sympathy for the printer and his wife; in an-instant, however, it was seized with an idea, and in the next instant it had acted upon it. Scarcely had the spirit of the little baby left its body, than the spirit of the young girl entered it.

Now a gentle warmth suffused the form of the little child, natural colour came into its cheeks, it breathed quietly and regularly, and when the printer and his wife came back, they found their baby in a healthful sleep. As they stood amazed at the change in the countenance of the child, it opened its eyes and smiled upon them.

"The crisis is past!" cried the mother. "She is saved; and it is all because you stopped at the church instead of hurrying home, as you wished to do." The ghost of the young girl knew that this was true, and the baby smiled again.

It was eighteen years later and the printer's baby had grown into a beautiful young woman. From her early childhood she had been fond of visiting the church, and would spend hours among the tombs reading the inscriptions, and sometimes sitting by them, especially by the tomb of Sir Geoffrey of the Marle. There, when there was nobody by, she used to talk with the bishop's ghost.

Late one afternoon she came to the tomb with a happy smile on her face. "Holy father," she said, speaking softly through the crack, "are you not tired of staying so long in this tomb which is not your own?"

"Truly I am, daughter," said the bishop's ghost, "but I have no right to complain: I never come back here in the early morning without a feeling of the warmest gratitude to you for having given me a place of refuge. My greatest trouble is caused by the fear that the ghost of Sir Geoffrey of the Marle may some time choose to return. In that case I must give up to him his tomb. And then, where, oh where shall I go?"

"Holy father," whispered the girl, "do not trouble yourself; you shall have your own tomb again and need fear no one."

"How it that?" exclaimed the bishop's ghost. "Tell me quickly, daughter."

"This is the way of it" replied the young girl. "When the mason plastered up the crack under the lid of your tomb he seems to have been very careful about the front part of it, but he didn't take much pains with the back where his work wasn't likely to be seen, so that there the plaster has crumbled and loosened very much, and with a long pin from my hair I have picked out ever so much of it, and now there is a great crack at the back of the tomb where you can go in and come out, just as easily as you ever did. As soon as night shall fall you can leave this tomb and go into your own.

The bishop's ghost could scarcely speak for thankful emotions, and the happy young girl went home to the house of her father, a prosperous man, now the head-printer of the town.

The next evening the young girl went to the church and hurried to the bishop's tomb. Therein she found the bishop's ghost, happy and contented.

Sitting on a stone projection at the back of the tomb, she had a long conversation with the bishop's ghost, which, in gratitude for what she had done, gave her all manner of good advice and counsel. "Above all things, my dear daughter," said the bishop's ghost, "do not repeat your first great mistake; promise me that never will you die of love."

The young girl smiled. "Fear not, good father," she replied. "When I died of love, I was, in body and soul, but eighteen years old, and knew no better; now, although my body is but eighteen, my soul is thirty-six. Fear not, never again shall I die of love."

JOHN BARTINE'S WATCH

A STORY BY A PHYSICIAN

Ambrose Bierce

The exact time? Good God! my friend, why do you insist? One would think—but what does it matter; it is easily bedtime—isn't that near enough? But, here, if you must set your watch, take mine and see for yourself."

With that he detached his watch—a tremendously heavy, old-fashioned one—from the chain, and handed it to me; then turned away, and walking across the room to a shelf of books, began an examination of their backs. His agitation and evident distress surprised me; they appeared reasonless. Having set my watch by his, I stepped over to where he stood and said, "Thank you."

As he took his timepiece and reattached it to the guard I observed that his hands were unsteady. With a tact upon which I greatly prided myself, I sauntered carelessly to the sideboard and took some brandy and water; then, begging his pardon for my thoughtlessness, asked him to have some and went back to my seat by the fire, leaving him to help himself, as was our custom. He did so and presently joined me at the hearth, as tranquil as ever.

This odd little incident occurred in my apartment, where John Bartine was passing an evening. We had dined together at the club, had come home in a cab and—in short, everything had been done in the most prosaic way; and why John Bartine should break in upon the natural and established order of things to make himself spectacular with a display of emotion, apparently for his own entertainment, I could nowise understand. The more I thought of it, while his brilliant conversational gifts were commending themselves to my inattention, the more curious I grew, and of course had no difficulty in persuading myself that my curiosity was friendly solicitude. That is the disguise that curiosity usually assumes to evade resentment. So I ruined one of the finest sentences of his disregarded monologue by cutting it short without ceremony.

"John Bartine," I said, "you must try to forgive me if I am wrong, but with the light that I have at present I cannot concede your right to go all to pieces when asked the time o' night. I cannot admit that it is proper to experience a mysterious reluctance to look your own watch in the face and to cherish in my presence, without explanation, painful emotions which are denied to me, and which are none of my business."

To this ridiculous speech Bartine made no immediate reply, but sat looking gravely into the fire. Fearing that I had offended I was about to apologize and beg him to think no more about the matter, when looking me calmly in the eyes he said:

"My dear fellow, the levity of your manner does not at all disguise the hideous impudence of your demand; but happily I had already decided to tell you what you wish to know and no manifestation of your unworthiness to hear it shall alter my decision. Be good enough to give me your attention and you shall hear all about the matter.

"This watch," he said, "had been in my family for three generations before it fell to me. Its original owner, for whom it was made, was my great-grandfather, Bramwell Olcott Bartine, a wealthy planter of Colonial Virginia, and as stanch a Tory as ever lay awake nights contriving new kinds of maledictions for the head of Mr. Washington, and new methods of aiding and abetting good King George. One day this worthy gentleman had the deep misfortune to perform for his cause a service of capital importance which was not recognized as legitimate by those who suffered its disadvantages. It does not matter what it was, but among its minor consequences was my excellent ancestor's arrest one night in his own house by a party of Mr. Washington's rebels. He was permitted to say farewell to his weeping family, and was then marched away into the darkness which swallowed him up forever. Not the slenderest clew to his fate was ever found. After the war the most diligent inquiry and the offer of large rewards failed to turn up any of his captors or any fact concerning his disappearance. He had disappeared, and that was all."

Something in Bartine's manner that was not in his words—I hardly knew what it was—prompted me to ask:

"What is your view of the matter—of the justice of it?"

"My view of it," he flamed out, bringing his clenched hand down upon the table as if he had been in a public house dicing with blackguards—"my view of it is that it was a characteristically dastardly assassination by that damned traitor, Washington, and his ragamuffin rebels!"

For some minutes nothing was said: Bartine was recovering his temper, and I waited. Then I said:

"Was that all?"

"No—there was something else. A few weeks after my great-grandfather's arrest his watch was found lying on the porch at the front door of his dwelling. It was wrapped in a sheet of letter paper bearing the name of Rupert Bartine, his only son, my grandfather. I am wearing that watch."

Bartine paused. His usually restless black eyes were staring fixedly into the grate, a point of red light in each, reflected from the glowing coals. He seemed to have forgotten me. A sudden threshing of the branches of a tree outside one of the windows, and almost at the same instant a rattle of rain against the glass, recalled him to a sense of his surroundings. A storm had risen, heralded by a single gust of wind, and in a few moments the steady plash of the water on the pavement was distinctly heard. I hardly know why I relate this incident; it seemed somehow to have a certain significance and relevancy which I am unable now to discern. It at least added an element of seriousness, almost solemnity. Bartine resumed:

"I have a singular feeling toward this watch—a kind of affection for it; I like to have it about me, though partly from its weight, and partly for a reason I shall now explain, I seldom carry it. The reason is this: Every evening when I have it with me I feel an unaccountable desire to open and consult it, even if I can think of no reason for wishing to know the time. But if I yield to it, the moment my eyes rest upon the dial I am filled with a mysterious apprehension—a sense of imminent calamity. And this is the more insupportable the nearer it is to eleven o'clock—by this watch, no matter what the actual hour may be. After the hands have registered eleven the desire to look is gone; I am entirely indifferent. Then I can consult the thing as often as I like, with no more emotion than you feel in looking at your own. Naturally I have trained myself not to look at that watch in the evening before eleven; nothing could induce me. Your insistence this evening upset me a trifle. I felt very much as I suppose an opium-eater might feel if his yearning for his special and particular kind of hell were reinforced by opportunity and advice.

"Now that is my story, and I have told it in the interest of your trumpery science; but if on any evening hereafter you observe me wearing this damnable watch, and you have the thoughtfulness to ask me the hour, I shall beg leave to put you to the inconvenience of being knocked down."

His humor did not amuse me. I could see that in relating his delusion he was again somewhat disturbed. His concluding smile was positively ghastly, and his eyes had resumed something more than their old restlessness; they shifted hither and thither about the room with apparent aimlessness and I fancied had on a wild expression, such as is sometimes observed in cases of dementia. Perhaps this was my own imagination, but at any rate I was now persuaded that my friend was afflicted with a most singular and interesting monomania. Without, I trust, any abatement of my affectionate solicitude for him as a friend, I began to regard him as a patient, rich in possibilities of profitable study. Why not? Had he not described his delusion in the interest of science? Ah, poor fellow, he was doing more for science than he knew: not only his story but himself was in evidence. I should cure him if I could, of course, but first I should make a little experiment in psychology— nay, the experiment itself might be a step in his restoration.

"That is very frank and friendly of you, Bartine," I said cordially, "and I'm rather proud of your confidence. It is all very odd, certainly. Do you mind showing me the watch?"

He detached it from his waistcoat, chain and all, and passed it to me without a word. The case was of gold, very thick and strong, and singularly engraved. After closely examining the dial and observing that it was nearly twelve o'clock, I opened it at the back and was interested to observe an inner case of ivory, upon which was painted a miniature portrait in that exquisite and delicate manner which was in vogue during the eighteenth century.

"Why, bless my soul!" I exclaimed, feeling a sharp artistic delight—"how under the sun did you get that done? I thought miniature painting on ivory was a lost art."

"That," he replied, gravely smiling, "is not I; it is my excellent great-grandfather, the late Bramwell Olcott Bartine, Esquire, of Virginia. He was younger then than later—about my age, in fact. It is said to resemble me; do you think so?"

"Resemble you? I should say so! Barring the costume, which I suppose you to have assumed out of compliment to the art—or for *vraisemblance*, so to say—and the no mustache, that portrait is you in every feature, line, and expression."

No more was said at that time. Bartine took a book from the table and began reading. I heard outside the incessant plash of the rain in the street. There were occasional hurried footfalls on the sidewalks; and once a slower, heavier tread seemed to cease at my door—a policeman, I thought, seeking shelter in the doorway. The boughs of the trees tapped significantly on the window panes, as if asking for admittance. I remember it all through these years and years of a wiser, graver life.

Seeing myself unobserved, I took the old fashioned key that dangled from the chain and quickly turned back the hands of the watch a full hour; then, closing the case, I handed Bartine his property and saw him replace it on his person.

"I think you said," I began, with assumed carelessness, "that after eleven the sight of the dial no longer affects you. As it is now nearly twelve"—looking at my own timepiece—"perhaps, if you don't resent my pursuit of proof, you will look at it now."

He smiled good-humoredly, pulled out the watch again, opened it, an instantly sprang to his feet with a cry that Heaven has not had the mercy to permit me to forget! His eyes, their blackness strikingly intensified by the pallor of his face, were fixed upon the watch, which he clutched in both hands. For some time he remained in that attitude without uttering another sound; then, in a voice that I should not have recognized as his, he said:

"Damn you! it is two minutes to eleven!"

I was not unprepared for some such outbreak, and without rising replied, calmly enough:

"I beg your pardon; I must have misread your watch in setting my own by it."

He shut the case with a sharp snap and put the watch in his pocket. He looked at me and made an attempt to smile, but his lower lip quivered and he seemed unable to close his mouth. His hands, also, were shaking, and he thrust them, clenched, into the pockets of his sack-coat. The courageous spirit was manifestly endeavoring to subdue the coward body. The effort was too great; he began to sway from side to side, as from vertigo, and before I could spring from my chair to support him his knees gave way and he pitched awkwardly forward and fell upon his face. I sprang to assist him to rise; but when John Bartine rises we shall all rise.

The *post-mortem* examination disclosed nothing; every organ was normal and sound. But when the body had been prepared for burial a faint dark circle was seen to have developed around the neck; at least I was so assured by several persons who said they saw it, but of my own knowledge I cannot say if that was true.

Nor can I set limitations to the law of heredity. I do not know that in the spiritual world a sentiment or emotion may not survive the heart that held it, and seek expression in a kindred life, ages removed. Surely, if I were to guess at the fate of Bramwell Olcott Bartine, I should guess that he was hanged at eleven o'clock in the evening, and that he had been allowed several hours in which to prepare for the change.

As to John Bartine, my friend, my patient for five minutes, and—Heaven forgive me!—my victim for eternity, there is no more to say. He is buried, and his watch with him—I saw to that. May God rest his soul in Paradise, and the soul of his Virginian ancestor, if, indeed, they are two souls.

THE OPEN WINDOW

Saki (H. H. Munro)

"My aunt will be down presently, Mr. Nuttel," said a very self-possessed young lady of fifteen; "in the meantime you must try and put up with me."

Framton Nuttel endeavoured to say the correct something which should duly flatter the niece of the moment without unduly discounting the aunt that was to come. Privately he doubted more than ever whether these formal visits on a succession of total strangers would do much towards helping the nerve cure which he was supposed to be undergoing.

"I know how it will be," his sister had said when he was preparing to migrate to this rural retreat; "you will bury yourself down there and not speak to a living soul, and your nerves will be worse than ever from moping. I shall just give you letters of introduction to all the people I know there. Some of them, as far as I can remember, were quite nice."

Framton wondered whether Mrs. Sappleton, the lady to whom he was presenting one of the letters of introduction, came into the nice division.

"Do you know many of the people round here?" asked the niece, when she judged that they had had sufficient silent communion.

"Hardly a soul," said Framton. "My sister was staying here, at the rectory, you know, some four years ago, and she gave me letters of introduction to some of the people here."

He made the last statement in a tone of distinct regret.

"Then you know practically nothing about my aunt?" pursued the self-possessed young lady.

"Only her name and address," admitted the caller. He was wondering whether Mrs. Sappleton was in the married or widowed state. An indefinable something about the room seemed to suggest masculine habitation.

"Her great tragedy happened just three years ago," said the child; "that would be since your sister's time."

"Her tragedy?" asked Framton; somehow in this restful country spot tragedies seemed out of place.

"You may wonder why we keep that window wide open on an October afternoon," said the niece, indicating a large French window that opened on to a lawn.

"It is quite warm for the time of the year," said Framton; "but has that window got anything to do with the tragedy?"

"Out through that window, three years ago to a day, her husband and her two young brothers went off for their day's shooting. They never came back. In crossing the moor to their favorite snipe-shooting ground they were all three engulfed in a treacherous piece of bog. It had been that dreadful wet summer, you know, and places that were safe in other years gave way suddenly without warning. Their bodies were never recovered. That was the dreadful part of it." Here the child's voice lost its self-possessed note and became falteringly human. "Poor aunt always thinks that they will come back some day, they and the little brown spaniel that was lost with them, and walk in at that window just as they used to do. That is why the window is kept open every evening till it is quite dusk. Poor dear aunt, she has often told me how they went out, her husband with his white waterproof coat over his arm, and Ronnie, her youngest brother, singing 'Bertie, why do you bound?' as he always did to tease her, because she said it got on her nerves. Do you know, sometimes on still, quiet evenings like this I almost get a creepy feeling that they will all walk in through that window——"

She broke off with a little shudder. It was a relief to Framton when the aunt bustled into the room with a whirl of apologies for being late in making her appearance.

"I hope Vera has been amusing you?" she said.

"She has been very interesting," said Framton.

"I hope you don't mind the open window," said Mrs. Sappleton briskly; "my husband and brothers will be home directly from shooting, and they always come in this way. They've been out for snipe in the marshes to-day, so they'll make a fine mess over my poor carpets. So like you menfolks, isn't it?"

She rattled on cheerfully about the shooting and the scarcity of birds, and the prospects for duck in the winter. To Framton it was all purely horrible. He made a desperate but only partially successful effort to turn the talk on to a less ghastly topic; he was conscious that his hostess was giving him only a fragment of her attention, and her eyes were constantly straying past him to the open window and the lawn beyond. It was certainly an unfortunate coincidence that he should have paid his visit on this tragic anniversary.

"The doctors agree in ordering me complete rest, an absence

of mental excitement, and avoidance of anything in the nature of violent physical exercise," announced Framton, who labored under the tolerably wide-spread delusion that total strangers and chance acquaintances are hungry for the least detail of one's ailments and infirmities, their cause and cure. "On the matter of diet they are not so much in agreement," he continued.

"No?" said Mrs. Sappleton, in a voice which only replaced a yawn at the last moment. Then she suddenly brightened into alert attention—but not to what Framton was saying.

"Here they are at last!" she cried. "Just in time for tea, and don't they look as if they were muddy up to the eyes!"

Framton shivered slightly and turned toward the niece with a look intended to convey sympathetic comprehension. The child was staring out through the open window with dazed horror in her eyes. In a chill shock of nameless fear Framton swung round in his seat and looked in the same direction.

In the deepening twilight three figures were walking across the lawn towards the window; they all carried guns under their arms, and one of them was additionally burdened with a white coat hung over his shoulders. A tired brown spaniel kept close at their heels. Noiselessly they neared the house, and then a hoarse young voice chanted out of the dusk: "I said, Bertie, why do you bound?"

Framton grabbed wildly at his stick and hat; the hall-door, the gravel-drive, and the front gate were dimly noted stages in his headlong retreat. A cyclist coming along the road had to run into a hedge to avoid imminent collision.

"Here we are, my dear," said the bearer of the white mackintosh, coming in through the window; "fairly muddy, but most of it's dry. Who was that who bolted out as we came up?"

"A most extraordinary man, a Mr. Nuttel," said Mrs. Sappleton; "could only talk about his illness, and dashed off without a word of good-bye or apology when you arrived. One would think he had seen a ghost."

"I expect it was the spaniel," said the niece calmly; "he told me he had a horror of dogs. He was once hunted into a cemetery somewhere on the banks of the Ganges by a pack of pariah dogs, and had to spend the night in a newly dug grave with the creatures snarling and grinning and foaming just above him. Enough to make anyone lose their nerve."

Romance at short notice was her specialty.

LE VERT GALANT

Anonymous

*D*uring the long vacation, in the summer of 186-, I started on a walking tour through Normandy and the northern part of France. For long I had been planning this scheme, and delighted I was when at length I stood on "the other side of the water," burning with desire to commence immediately my travels and adventures. For many weeks I journeyed in the usual routine so well-known to pedestrians, and on which I shall therefore not enlarge; for nothing worthy of note occurred until the story I am about to relate, which is certainly out of the common.

One summer's evening, having been walking all day, I was not sorry when, looking down from the hill I had just reached, I discovered through the deepening twilight, at about the distance of a mile, the quaint-looking village of H—— in the valley beneath me. The *entourage* was picturesque in the extreme; and behind the village, making a dark background, rose a sombre-looking pine-wood.

I put my best foot foremost; though, to say the honest truth, there was not much to choose between the two, for I was very weary; and thankful I was when I found myself walking up the quaint paved street, on the look-out for the best inn. Yes, there it stood—that must be it—rather aloof from its neighbours, with its gable-ends and old-fashioned colouring, and the sign-board over the door. "Le Vert Galant" it called itself; and a picture of "Le Galant," dressed in a green coat, rather in the Henri-IV. style, hung over the door, and grinned down on me with a stern welcome.

I entered and asked if I could have a night's lodgings there. I was met by the landlady, a handsome and still young-looking woman, her dress betokening her a widow. She courteously invited me in, and, showing me into a room up one pair of stairs, informed me that Nanette, the waiting-maid, should come and announce to me when my supper was *servi*.

I unpacked my knapsack and performed my hasty toilette, thoroughly enjoying the transition from my thick walking-boots to my slippers. Then I gazed out the window. It looked upon a large old-fashioned garden, thick with flowers, whose drowsy incense filled the air with sweetness. I was charmed with my window, surrounded as it was with ivy; and fully did I sympathize and share in the feelings of any owl who had as charming an ivy-bush as mine. Running down close to my window was a pipe or *goutière*, which caught all the rainwater in a barrel below. "Hurrah!" said I to myself, "soft water into the bargain." In one corner of the garden stood an old-fashioned pump, looking rather green and mouldy, as if it thought itself quite neglected. I was thus musing and thinking how impossible it would be to render adequately the gorgeous colours of the flowers below me on paper (for I was a dabbler in colours myself, and managed to spoil a good deal of paper), when Nanette, tapping briskly at my door, announced my *soupé*. I descended into the comfortable kitchen; for madame, like a sensible woman, surmised I should prefer the snug warm room to a cold cheerless parlour, which could not be warmed in a moment.

I discussed my supper with considerable pleasure, madame again showing her good sense by leaving me quiet until I had taken off the edge of my appetite; and, my meal over, she pointed to a stool in the chimney-corner, saying that if it was not too hot for me, I should find it comfortable; adding also that "c'était permis de fumer dans la cuisine." Charming woman! What more could the heart of man wish for? She seated herself opposite to me with her knitting, and began telling me (while I smoked) about the village, the people who lived in it, and finally herself; how she had been left early a widow, with one daughter, by name "Justine." Ah, so pretty! but very ailing and weak at present. She continued thus chatting until I rose to go to bed, when she lighted me upstairs, and bade me good-night.

I suppose I must have been overtired by my long walk; anyhow sleep refused to "steep my senses in forgetfulness;" so I got up, and with a sort of vague attraction I walked to the window. I have already said that my room looked out into an old-fashioned garden, with a wall running round it, and, instead of a path of gravel or sand, there was a narrow red-brick alley or *trottoir*. I peeped out of my ivy-surrounded window. There was not a leaf stirring. The garden looked white and cold in the glistening moonlight. All still, I thought to myself; no life. All the world, save myself, peacefully sleeping. No, that was not quite the case; for, looking beyond the ivy in the garden below, I saw the figure of a young girl, in the old Normandy dress—high cap and sabots. She was pumping slowly, slowly at the old pump before mentioned, which stood in the corner—so mechanically that she appeared to me to be a part of a piece of machinery. I only saw her back. She was entirely in the shadow of the wall, except when her long arms rose with the handle, and flashed white and gleaming for a moment in the moonlight. There was a sort of fascination about her. I *could* not help watching her; but what struck me as odd was that though she pumped and the water ran into the trough below, I could not hear the slightest noise. I gazed again, my artistic eye took it all in, and I thought (not without half a shudder) what a pretty picture she would make, standing there, with the moon above, casting long shadows—still and quiet—upon every object in the garden. I looked for the shadow of the pump—there it was, and the handle working up and down across a bed of roses; but apparently it was working of its own accord. I looked for the girl; there she stood, working in the same mechanical way, but *she had no shadow.*

A horrible dread of something supernatural now came over me. I stared at her again, when, just at that moment, I was conscious of a stir in the ivy around my window, and then, with a swift sliding movement (the ivy gently sighing in response), I saw a dark object swing itself down the *goutière* or pipe, close to my window, and land below, beside the black tarred barrel. Looking down, I saw a fine strong young man rise and walk, heedless of the garden-beds, straight toward the pump. On getting within a few paces of the girl (she still continuing her unearthly pumping) he raised his hat, a sort of *chapeau brigand* and I discerned in the ever-varying moonlight a clear-cut handsome profile, slightly bent in salutation. He replaced his hat and held out his hand. No word of greeting passed either of their lips. For the first time *she* turned, and O, what a wan weird face gleamed on his! She took his offered hand, and so they walked down the red brick-path—her sabots (the first sound I had heard) making a hollow click-clack along the *trottoir.* They reached the old green door in the wall, which, responsive to his pull, groaned itself open. She passed through. He half turned and looked back at the old house, then he followed her, and the old door shut again with a resounding bang.

Having partially recovered myself after this horrible and ghostly scene, which seemed to freeze the marrow of my bones, I went to bed, and passed a most disturbed night, mixed up with dreams of pumps and sabots, and I was thankful when morning broke, and I rose.

I packed up my knapsack, and then called Nanette, intending to order my breakfast and get away from this inn, whose very atmosphere now made me shudder; but first I must question Nanette, and get out of her the true story—for story I felt sure there was—of the haunted inn.

Nanette appeared, looking extremely coquettish in a small cap and cherry-coloured bows, and cheerfully hoped monsieur had slept well, and what would he have for his breakfast. I hardly answered her; going straight to the point, I said,

"Nanette, is that pump in the corner of the garden ever used?"

Her countenance fell as she replied,

"But very rarely, monsieur; why?"

"Does your mistress keep any other maid but yourself?"

"Mais non."

I could not help noticing her face of growing alarm.

"Then," I said calmly, "who was that girl I saw last night pumping there with a high cap and sabots?"

Nanette started forward, and caught me by the arm.

"Dites donc que vous ne l'avez pas vu?" said she.

Hardly had the words escaped her lips, when through the house there rang a piercing wailing shriek, and a voice from a neighbouring room cried, "Nanette, Nanette, je meurs!"

Nanette stood stock-still listening, with her lips parted, her arm raised, then exclaiming, "Ciel! c'est accompli déjà!" rushed out of the room. I could not help following her. On the landing she met madame; Nanette made but one step to her, and whispered (but I caught the whisper), "Il l'a vu," indicating me by an expressive thumb pointed over her shoulder.

"Qui?" said madame.

"Susanne."

Madame, on hearing this reply, sat down on the top step of the stairs, and gave herself over to what I thought premature and unnecessary grief, interspersed with ejaculations of "O, mon enfant, que le bon Dieu te prenne aux cieux!"

Meanwhile I had followed Nanette into a room along the passage, and on entering I saw a young girl half sitting, half lying, in bed, struggling to catch her failing breath; the window was thrown wide open, and the scent of those spell-stricken flowers streaming up through it.

I plainly saw she was dying fast. I looked at her again; the face seemed strangely familiar to me—and yet where could I have seen her?

Just then madame entered; the young girl raised herself, and said feebly, "Chère mère, adieu, je pars!" She held up her face to be kissed, and I caught her upturned side face. The likeness flashed upon me like a thunderbolt. She was the living image of that ghostly figure in the *chapeau brigand* that I had watched in the garden the night before.

Justine (for she it was who lay a-dying) whispered, "Pray for me—pray!"

Madame, in an agony, looked at me, and in a strangled voice, said:

"Say just one little prayer for my poor child—for me; I lose my head."

I came near the bed, close to Justine, and repeated an old French prayer which fortunately at that moment came into my head. Hardly was it over when Justine raised herself in bed, with eyes straining at something beyond mortal ken, and, as if in answer to some unheard call, said "Je viens!" fell back and died.

Was it *only* imagination? or did I really at that moment hear, through the open window, the sound of a hollow footfall in a sabot—click-clack all down the *trottoir*—and then the garden-door bang? I think not.

I was so overwhelmed by all these strange occurrences, that, after leaving poor Justine's room, I sallied forth to stroll by the river and collect my scattered senses. I thought it all over—the strange apparitions of the previous night, Nanette's face of horror at my mention of them, and subsequently Justine's sudden death. Yes, I must get to the bottom of all this before leaving the village, which I fixed to do that afternoon; so I returned and had an interview with madame, who was very kind, though heartbroken at Justine's death. She said it was no good concealing from me the story that overshadowed the inn, and as I was soon going, perhaps I should like to hear it. On my acquiescing at once, she led the way into the kitchen, and sitting down, she related the narrative, of which this is the epitome.

It appears that Le Vert Galant had for some generations belonged to the same family, and had always been handed down from father to son; eventually madame's husband had come into possession thereof. But it was of one of his ancestors that I would speak, who lived in this inn, and rejoiced in a large family of both sons and daughters. One of the former fell very much in love with a pretty girl living in the village; but the match was disapproved by all the parents, so that the lovers had to meet clandestinely.

When this girl—Susanne by name—could slip away unobserved, she used to give the sign, before agreed upon between the two, of running into the old garden of the inn and pumping; on hearing which welcome sound, Jacques, a strong able-bodied young man, would swing himself down from his window by the *goutière*, and so, unperceived, they used to wander into the adjoining pine-wood.

But one evening, the tryst having been accomplished as usual, they sallied forth, and once in the sheltering pine-wood, Susanne turned round on her lover and upbraided him bitterly with a decrease of affection for her, and then the usual lovers' quarrel ensued. Swift angry words passed on both sides, till Jacques, goaded almost to madness by her reproaches, and being also of a very hasty temper, drew out his knife, and without a moment's hesitation stabbed her to the heart. No sooner was the deed done than O, how bitterly was it repented of! He threw himself on the ground by her side, and by every endearing name strove to recall that life which his own hand had taken; but all of no avail. Then he began to think of the consequences: what would become of him? what would his parents say? He rose and wandered miles and miles, pursued by revengeful phantoms, all the creation of his overwrought brain, till finally, coming to the edge of a dangerous precipice, he recklessly flung himself over, and thus ended his own miserable existence.

But as surely as any of his family die, so surely is the event foreshadowed by the ghostly appearance of his murdered Susanne in the garden, bidding her lover to the well-known tryst; and his spirit answering her summons, they react together the horrible tragedy which time cannot obliterate or years efface.

That afternoon, with many expressions of sympathy, I took my leave of madame and of the village of H——, mentally resolving that, should fortune at any future time conduct my steps thither, I would avoid that old haunted inn—Le Vert Galant.

ON THE RIVER

From the French of **Guy de Maupassant**
Translated by **Jonathan Sturges**

I had rented, last summer, a little country house on the banks of the Seine a few miles from Paris, and I used to go down there every night to sleep. In a few days I made the acquaintance of one of my neighbors, a man between thirty and forty, who was certainly the most curious type that I had ever met. He was an old rowing man, crazy about rowing, always near the water, always on the water, always in the water. He must have been born in a boat, and he would certainly die in a boat at last.

One night, while we were walking together along the Seine, I asked him to tell me some stories about his life upon the river; and at that the good man suddenly became animated, transfigured, eloquent, almost poetical! In his heart there was one great passion, devouring and irresistible—the river.

"Ah!" said he to me, "how many memories I have of that river which is flowing there beside us. You people who live in streets, you don't know what the river is. But just listen to a fisherman simply pronouncing the word. For him it is the thing mysterious, the thing profound, unknown, the country of mirage and of phatasmagoria, where one sees, at night, things which do not exist, where one hears strange noises, where one trembles causelessly, as though crossing a graveyard. And it is, indeed, the most sinister of graveyards—a graveyard where there are no tombstones.

"To the fisherman the land seems limited, but of dark nights, when there is no moon, the river seems limitless. Sailors have no such feeling for the sea. Hard she often is and wicked, the great Sea; but she cries, she shouts, she deals with you fairly, while the river is silent and treacherous. It never even mutters, it flows ever noiselessly, and this eternal flowing movement of water terrifies me far more than the high seas of ocean.

"Dreamers pretend that the Sea hides in her breast great blue regions where drowned men roll to and fro among the huge fish, in the midst of strange forests and in crystal grottos. The river has only black depths, where one rots in the slime. For all that it is beautiful when it glitters in the rising sun or swashes softly along between its banks where the reeds murmur.

"The poet says of the ocean:

" 'Oh seas, you know sad stories! Deep seas, feared by kneeling mothers, you tell the stories to one another at flood tides! And that is why you have such despairing voices when at night you come towards us nearer and nearer.'

"Well, I think that the stories murmured by the slender reeds with their little soft voices must be yet more sinister than the gloomy dramas told by the howling of the high seas.

"But, since you ask for some of my recollections, I will tell you a curious adventure which I had here about ten years ago.

"I then lived, as I still do, in the house of the old lady Lafon, and one of my best chums, Louis Bernet, who has now given up for the Civil Service his oars, his low shoes, and his sleeveless jersey, lived in the village of C——, two leagues farther down. We dined together every day—sometimes at his place, sometimes at mine.

"One evening as I was returning home alone and rather tired, wearily pulling my heavy boat, a twelve-footer, which I always used at night, I stopped a few seconds to take breath near the point where so many reeds grow, down that way, about two hundred metres before you come to the railroad bridge. It was a beautiful night; the moon was resplendent, the river glittered, the air was calm and soft. The tranquility of it all tempted me; I said to myself that to smoke a pipe just here would be extremely nice. Action followed upon the thought; I seized my anchor and threw it into the stream.

"The boat, which floated down again with the current, pulled the chain out to its full length, then stopped; and I seated myself in the stern on a sheepskin, as comfortable as possible. One heard no sound—no sound; only sometimes I thought I was aware of a low, almost insensible lapping of the water along the band, and I made out some groups of reeds which, taller than their fellows, took on surprising shapes, and seemed from time to time to stir.

"The river was perfectly still, but I felt myself moved by the extraordinary silence which surrounded me. All the animals—the frogs and toads, those nocturnal singers of the marshes—were silent. Suddenly on my right, near me, a frog croaked; I started; it was silent; I heard nothing more, and I resolved to smoke a little by way of a distraction. But though I am, so to speak, a regular blackener of pipes, I could not smoke that night; after the second puff I sickened of it, and I stopped. I began to hum a tune; the sound of my voice was painful to me; so I stretched myself out in the bottom of the boat and contemplated the sky. For some time I remained quiet, but soon the slight movements of the boat began to make me uneasy. I thought that it was yawing tremendously, striking now this bank of the stream, and now that; then I thought that some Being or some invisible force was dragging it down gently to the bottom of the water, and then was lifting it up simply to let it fall again. I was tossed about as though in the midst of a storm; I heard noises all around me; with a sudden start I sat upright; the water sparkled, everything was calm.

"I saw that my nerves were unsettled, and I decided to go. I pulled in the chain; the boat moved; then I was conscious of resistance; I pulled harder; the anchor did not come up, it had caught on something at the bottom of the river and I could not lift it. I pulled again—in vain. With my oars I got the boat round upstream in order to change the position of the anchor. It was no use; the anchor still held. I grew angry, and in a rage I shook the chain. Nothing moved. There was no hope of breaking the chain, or of getting it loose from my craft, because it was very heavy, and riveted at the bow into a bar of wood thicker than my arm; but since the weather continued fine, I reflected that I should not have to wait long before meeting some fisherman, who would come to my rescue. My mishap had calmed me; I sat down, and was able to smoke my pipe. I had a flask of brandy with me; I drank two or three glasses, and my situation made me laugh. It was very hot, so that, if needs must, I could pass the night under the stars without inconvenience.

"Suddenly a little knock sounded against the side. I started, and a cold perspiration froze me from head to foot. The noise came, no doubt, from some bit of wood drawn along by the current, but it was enough, and I felt myself again overpowered by a strange nervous agitation. I seized the chain, and I stiffened myself in a desperate effort. The anchor held. I sat down exhausted.

"But, little by little, the river had covered itself with a very thick white mist, which crept low over the water, so that, standing up, I could no longer see either the stream or my feet or my boat, and saw only the tips of the reeds, and then, beyond them, the

plain, all pale in the moonlight, and with great black stains which
rose towards heaven, and which were made by clumps of Italian
poplars. I was as though wrapped to the waist in a cotton sheet of
strange whiteness, and there began to come to me weird imagina-
tions. I imagined that some one was trying to climb into my boat,
since I could no longer see it, and that the river, hidden by this
opaque mist, must be full of strange creatures swimming about
me. I experienced a horrible uneasiness, I had a tightening at the
temples, my heart beat to suffocation; and, losing my head, I
thought of escaping by swimming; then in an instant the very idea
made me shiver with fright. I saw myself lost, drifting hither and
thither in this impenetrable mist, struggling among the long grass
and the reeds which I should not be able to avoid, with a rattle in
my throat from fear, not seeing the shore, not finding my boat.
And it seemed to me as though I felt myself being drawn by the
feet down to the bottom of this black water.

"In fact, since I should have had to swim up stream at least five
hundred metres before finding a point clear of rushes and reeds,
where I could get a footing, there were nine chances to one that,
however good a swimmer I might be, I should lose my bearing in
the fog and drown.

"I tried to reason with myself. I realized that my will was firmly
enough resolved against fear; but there was something in me
beside my will, and it was this which felt afraid. I asked myself
what it could be that I dreaded; that part of me which was courageous railed at that part of me which was cowardly; and I never
had comprehended so well before the opposition between those
two beings which exist within us, the one willing, the other resist-
ing, and each in turn getting the mastery.

"This stupid and inexplicable fear grew until it became terror.
I remained motionless, my eyes wide open, with a strained and
expectant ear. Expecting—what? I did not know save that it would

be something terrible. I believe that if a fish, as often happens, had taken it into its head to jump out of the water, it would have needed only that to make me fall stark on my back into a faint.

"And yet, finally, by a violent effort, I very nearly recovered the reason which had been escaping me. I again took my brandy-flask, and out of it I drank great draughts. Then an idea struck me, and I began to shout with all my might, turning in succession towards all four quarters of the horizon. When my throat was completely paralyzed, I listened. A dog howled, a long way off.

"Again I drank; and I lay down on my back in the bottom of the boat. So I remained for one hour, perhaps for two, sleepless, my eyes wide-open, with nightmares all about me. I did not dare to sit up, and yet I had a wild desire to do so; I kept putting it off from minute to minute. I would say to myself: "Come! get up!" and I was afraid to make a movement. At last I raised myself with infinite precaution, as if life depended on my making not the slightest sound, and I peered over the edge of the boat.

"I was dazzled by the most marvellous, the most astonishing spectacle that it can be possible to see. It was one of those phantasmagoria from fairy-land; it was one of those visions described by travellers returned out of far countries, and which we hear without believing.

"The mist, which two hours before was floating over the water, had gradually withdrawn and piled itself upon the banks. Leaving the river absolutely clear, it had formed, along each shore, long low hills about six or seven metres high, which glittered under the moon with the brilliancy of snow, so that one saw nothing except this river of fire coming down these two white mountains; and there, high above my head, a great, luminous moon, full and large, displayed herself upon a blue and milky sky.

"All the denizens of the water had awaked; the bull-frogs croaked furiously, while, from instant to instant, now on my right, now on my left, I heard those short, mournful, monotonous notes which the brassy voices of the marsh-frogs give forth to the stars. Strangely enough, I was no longer afraid; I was in the midst of such an extraordinary landscape that the most curious things could not have astonished me.

"How long the sight lasted I do not know, because at last I had grown drowsy. When I again opened my eyes the moon had set, the heaven was full of clouds. The water lashed mournfully, the wind whispered, it grew cold, the darkness was profound.

"I drank all the brandy I had left; then I listened shiveringly to the rustling of the reeds and to the sinister noise of the river. I tried to see, but I could not make out the boat nor even my own hands, though I raised them close to my eyes.

"However, little by little the density of the blackness diminished. Suddenly I thought I felt a shadow slipping along near by me; I uttered a cry; a voice replied—it was a fisherman. I hailed him; he approached, and I told him of my mishap. He pulled his boat alongside, and both together we heaved at the chain. The anchor did not budge. The day came on—sombre, gray, rainy, cold—one of those days which bring always a sorrow and a misfortune. I made out another craft; we hailed it. The man aboard of it joined his efforts to ours, then, little by little, the anchor yielded. It came up, slowly, slowly, and weighted down by something very heavy. At last we perceived a black mass, and we pulled it along-side.

"It was the corpse of an old woman with a great stone round her neck."

THE CONSIDERATE HOSTS

Thorp McClusky

MIDNIGHT.

It was raining, abysmally. Not the kind of rain in which people sometimes fondly say they like to walk, but rain that was heavy and pitiless, like the rain that fell in France during the war. The road, unrolling slowly beneath Marvin's headlights, glistened like the flank of a great backsnake; almost Marvin expected it to writhe out from beneath the wheels of his car. Marvin's small coupe was the only man-made thing that moved through the seething night.

Within the car, however, it was like a snug little cave. Marvin might almost have been in a theater, unconcernedly watching some somber drama in which he could revel without really being touched. His sensation was almost one of creepiness; it was incredible that he could be so close to the rain and still so warm and dry. He hoped devoutly that he would not have a flat tire on a night like this!

Ahead a tiny red pinpoint appeared at the side of the road, grew swiftly, then faded in the car's glare to the bull's-eye of a lantern, swinging in the gloved fist of a big man in a streaming rubber coat. Marvin automatically braked the car and rolled the right-hand window down a little way as he saw the big man come splashing toward him.

"Bridge's washed away," the big man said. "Where you going, Mister?"

"Felders, damn it!"

"You'll have to go around by Little Rock Falls. Take your left up that road. It's a county road, but it's passable. Take your right after you cross Little Rock Falls bridge again. It'll bring you into Felders."

Marvin swore. The trooper's face, black behind the ribbons of water dripping from his hat, laughed.

"It's a bad night, Mister."

"Gosh, yes! Isn't it!"

Well, if he must detour, he must detour. What a night to crawl for miles along a rutty back road.

Rutty was no word for it. Every few feet Marvin's car plunged into water-filled holes, gouged out from beneath by the settling of the light roadbed. The sharp, cutting sound of loose stone against the tires was audible even above the hiss of the rain.

Four miles, and Marvin's motor began to sputter and cough. Another mile, and it surrendered entirely. The ignition was soaked; the car would not budge.

Marvin peered through the moisture-streaked windows, and, vaguely, like blacker masses beyond the road, he sensed the presence of thickly clustered trees. The car had stopped in the middle of a little patch of woods. "Judas!" Marvin thought disgustedly. "What a swell place to get stalled!" He switched off the lights to save the battery.

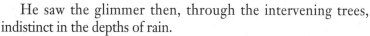

He saw the glimmer then, through the intervening trees, indistinct in the depths of rain.

Where there was a light there was certainly a house, and perhaps a telephone. Marvin pulled his hat tightly down upon his head, clasped his coat collar up around his ears, got out of the car, pushed the small coupe over on the shoulder of the road, and ran for the light.

The house stood perhaps twenty feet back from the road, and the light shone from a front-room window. As he plowed through the muddy yard—there was no sidewalk—Marvin noticed a second stalled car—a big sedan—standing black and deserted a little way down the road.

The rain was beating him, soaking him to the skin; he pounded on the house door like an impatient sheriff. Almost instantly the door swung open, and Marvin saw a man and a woman standing just inside, in a little hallway that led directly into a well-lighted living-room.

The hallway itself was quite dark. And the man and woman were standing close together, almost as though they might be endeavoring to hide something behind them. But Marvin, wholly preoccupied with his own plight, failed to observe how unusual it must be for these two rural people to be up and about, fully dressed, long after midnight.

Partly shielded from the rain by the little overhang above the door, Marvin took off his dripping hat and urgently explained his plight.

"My car. Won't go. Wires wet, I guess. I wonder if you'd let me use your phone? I might be able to get somebody to come out from Little Rock Falls. I'm sorry that I had to——"

"That's all right," the man said. "Come inside. When you knocked at the door you startled us. We—we really hadn't—well, you know how it is, in the middle of the night and all. But come in."

"We'll have to think this out differently, John," the woman said suddenly.

Think what out differently? thought Marvin absently.

Marvin muttered something about you never can be too careful about strangers, what with so many hold-ups and all. And, oddly, he sensed that in the half darkness the man and woman smiled briefly at each other, as though they shared some secret that made any conception of physical danger to themselves quietly, mildly amusing.

"We weren't thinking of you in that way," the man reassured Marvin. "Come into the living-room."

The living-room of that house was—just ordinary. Two overstuffed chairs, a davenport, a bookcase. Nothing particularly modern about the room. Not elaborate, but adequate.

In the brighter light Marvin looked at his hosts. The man was around forty years of age, the woman considerably younger, twenty-eight, or perhaps thirty. And there was something definitely attractive about them. It was not their appearance so much, for in appearance they were merely ordinary people; the woman was almost painfully plain. But they moved and talked with a curious singleness of purpose. They reminded Marvin of a pair of gray doves.

Marvin looked around the room until he saw the telephone in a corner, and he noticed with some surprise that it was one of the old-style, coffee-grinder affairs. The man was watching him with peculiar intentness.

"We haven't tried to use the telephone tonight," he told Marvin abruptly, "but I'm afraid it won't work."

"I don't see how it *can* work," the woman added.

Marvin took the receiver off the hook and rotated the little crank. No answer from Central. He tried again, several times, but the line remained dead.

The man nodded his head slowly. "I didn't think it would work," he said, then.

"Wires down or something, I suppose," Marvin hazarded. "Funny thing, I haven't seen one of these old-style phones in years. Didn't think they used 'em any more."

"You're out in the sticks now," the man laughed. He glanced from the window at the almost opaque sheets of rain falling outside.

"You might as well stay here a little while. While you're with us you'll have the illusion, at least, that you're in a comfortable house."

What on earth is he talking about? Marvin asked himself. Is he just a little bit off, maybe? The last sounded like nonsense.

Suddenly the woman spoke.

"He'd better go, John. He can't stay here too long, you know. It would be horrible if someone took his license number and people—jumped to conclusions afterward. No one should know that he stopped here."

The man looked thoughtfully at Marvin.

"Yes, dear, you're right. I hadn't thought that far ahead. I'm afraid, sir, that you'll have to leave," he told Marvin. "Something extremely strange——"

Marvin bristled angrily, and buttoned his coat with an air of affronted dignity.

"I'll go," he said shortly. "I realize perfectly that I'm an intruder. You should have not let me in. After you let me in I began to expect ordinary human courtesy from you. I was mistaken. Good night."

The man stopped him. He seemed very much distressed.

"Just a moment. Don't go until we explain. We have never been considered discourteous before. But tonight—tonight . . .

"I must introduce myself. I am John Reed, and this is my wife, Grace."

He paused significantly, as though that explained everything, but Marvin merely shook his head. "My name's Marvin Phelps, but that's nothing to you. All this talk seems pretty needless."

The man coughed nervously. "Please understand. We're only asking you to go for your own good."

"Oh, sure," Marvin said. "Sure. I understand perfectly. Good night."

The man hesitated. "You see," he said slowly, "things aren't as they seem. We're really ghosts."

"You don't say!"

"My husband is quite right," the woman said loyally. "We've been dead twenty-one years."

"Twenty-two years next October," the man added, after a moment's calculation. "It's a long time."

"Well, I never heard such hooey!" Marvin babbled. "Kindly step away from that door, Mister, and let me out of here before I swing from the heels!"

"I know it sounds odd," the man admitted, without moving, "and I hope that you will realize that it's from no choosing of mine that I have to explain. Nevertheless, I was electrocuted, twenty-one years ago, for the murder of the Chairman of the School Board, over in Little Rock Falls. Notice how my head is shaved, and my split trouser-leg? The fact is, that whenever we materialize we have to appear exactly as we were in our last moment of life. It's a restriction on us."

Screwy, certainly screwy. And yet Marvin hazily remembered that School Board affair. Yes, the murderer *had* been a fellow named Reed. The wife had committed suicide a few days after burial of her husband's body.

It was such an odd insanity. Why, they *both* believed it. They even dressed the part. That odd dress the woman was wearing. Way out of date. And the man's slit trouser-leg. The screwy cluck

97

had even shaved a little patch on his head, too, and his shirt was open at the throat.

They didn't look dangerous, but you never can tell. Better humor them, and get out of here as quick as I can.

Marvin cleared his throat.

"If I were you—why, say, I'd have lots of fun materializing. I'd be at it every night. Build up a reputation for myself."

The man looked disgusted. "I should kick you out of doors," he remarked bitterly. "I'm trying to give you a decent explanation, and you keep making fun of me."

"Don't bother with him, John," the wife exclaimed. "It's getting late."

"Mr. Phelps," the self-styled ghost doggedly persisted, ignoring the woman's interruption, "perhaps you noticed a car stalled on the side of the road as you came into our yard. Well, that car, Mr. Phelps, belongs to Lieutenant-Governor Lyons, of Felders, who prosecuted me for that murder and won a conviction, although he knew that I was innocent. Of course he wasn't Lieutenant-Governor then; he was only County Prosecutor. . . .

"That was a political murder, and Lyons knew it. But at that time he still had his way to make in the world—and circumstances pointed toward me. For example, the body of the slain man was found in the ditch just beyond my house. The body had been robbed. The murderer had thrown the victim's pocketbook and watch under our front steps. Lyons said that I had *hidden* them there—though obviously I'd never have done a suicidal thing like that, had I really been the murderer. Lyons knew that, too—but he had to burn somebody.

"What really convicted me was the fact that my contract to teach had not been renewed that spring. It gave Lyons a ready-made motive to pin on me.

"So he framed me. They tried, sentenced, and electrocuted

me, all very neatly and legally. Three days after I was buried, my wife committed suicide."

Though Marvin was a trifle afraid, he was nevertheless beginning to enjoy himself. Boy, what a story to tell the gang! If only they'd believe him!

"I can't understand," he pointed out slyly, "how you can be so free with this house if, as you say, you've been dead twenty-one years or so. Don't the present owners or occupants object? If I lived here I certainly wouldn't turn the place over to a couple of ghosts—especially on a night like this!"

The man answered readily, "I told you that things are not as they seem. This house has not been lived in since Grace died. It's not a very modern house, anyway—and people have natural prejudices. At this very moment you are standing in an empty room. Those windows are broken. The wallpaper has peeled away, and half the plaster has fallen off the walls. There is really no light in the house. If things appeared to you as they really are you could not see your hand in front of your face."

Marvin felt in his pocket for his cigarettes. "Well," he said, "you seem to know all the answers. Have a cigarette. Or don't ghosts smoke?"

The man extended his hand. "Thanks," he replied. "This is an unexpected pleasure. You'll notice that although there are ashtrays about the room there are no cigarettes or tobacco. Grace never smoked, and when they took me to jail she brought all my tobacco there to me. Of course, as I pointed out before, you see this room exactly as it was at the time she killed herself. She's wearing the same dress, for example. There's a certain form about these things, you know."

Marvin lit the cigarettes. "Well!" he exclaimed. "Brother, you certainly seem to think of everything! Though I can't understand, even yet, why you want me to get out of here. I should think that after you've gone to all this trouble, arranging your effects and so on, you'd want somebody to haunt."

The woman laughed dryly.

"Oh, you're not the man we want to haunt, Mr. Phelps. You came along quite by accident; we hadn't counted on you at all. No, Mr. Lyons is the man we're interested in."

"He's out in the hall now," the man said suddenly. He jerked his head toward the door through which Marvin had come. And all at once all this didn't seem half so funny to Marvin as it had seemed a moment before.

"You see," the woman went on quickly, "this house of ours is on a back road. Nobody ever travels this way. We've been trying for years to—to haunt Mr. Lyons, but we've had very little success. He lives in Felders, and we're pitifully weak when we go to Felders. We're strongest when we're in this house, perhaps because we lived here so long.

"But tonight, when the bridge went out, we knew that our opportunity had arrived. We knew that Mr. Lyons was not in Felders, and we knew that he would have to take this detour in order to get home.

"We felt very strongly that Mr. Lyons would be unable to pass this house tonight.

"It turned out as we had hoped. Mr. Lyons had trouble with his car, exactly as you did, and he came straight to this house to ask if he might use the telephone. Perhaps he had forgotten us, years ago—twenty-one years is a long time. Perhaps he was confused by the rain, and didn't know exactly where he was.

"He fainted, Mr. Phelps, the instant he recognized us. We have known for a long time that his heart is weak, and we had hoped that seeing us would frighten him to death, but he is still alive. Of course while he is unconscious we can do nothing more. Actually, we're almost impalpable. If you weren't so convinced that we are real you could pass your hand right through us.

"We decided to wait until Mr. Lyons regained consciousness and then to frighten him again. We even discussed beating him to death with one of those non-existent chairs you think you see. You understand, his body would be unmarked; he would really die of terror. We were still discussing what to do when you came along.

"We realized at once how embarrassing it might prove for you if Mr. Lyons' body were found in this house tomorrow and the police learned that you were also in the house. That's why we want you to go."

"Well," Marvin said bluntly. "I don't see how I can get my car away from here. It won't run, and if I walk to Little Rock Falls and get somebody to come back here with me the damage'll be done."

"Yes," the man admitted thoughtfully. "It's a problem."

For several minutes they stood like a tableau, without speaking. Marvin was uneasily wondering: Did these people really have old Lyons tied up in the hallway; were they really planning to murder the man? The big car standing out beside the road belonged to *somebody*. . . .

Marvin coughed discreetly.

"Well, it seems to me, my dear shades," he said, "that unless you are perfectly willing to put me into what might turn out to be a very unpleasant position you'll have to let your vengeance ride, for tonight, anyway."

"There'll never be another opportunity like this," the man pointed out. "That bridge won't go again in ten lifetimes."

"We don't want the young man to suffer though, John."

"It seems to me," Marvin suggested, "as though this revenge idea of yours is overdone, anyway. Murdering Lyons won't really do you any good, you know."

"It's the customary thing when a wrong has been done," the man protested.

"Well, maybe," Marvin argued, and all the time he was wondering whether he were really facing a madman who might be dangerous or whether he were at home dreaming in bed; "but I'm not so sure about that. Hauntings are pretty infrequent, you must admit. I'd say that shows that a lot of ghosts really don't care much about the vengeance angle, despite all you say. I think that if you check on it carefully you'll find that a great many ghosts realize that revenge isn't so much. It's really the thinking about revenge, and the planning it, that's all the fun. Now, for the sake of argument, what good would it do you to put old Lyons away? Why, you'd hardly have any incentive to be ghosts any more. But if you let him go, why, say, any time you wanted to, you could start to scheme up a good scare for him, and begin to calculate how it would work, and time would fly like everything. And on top of all that, if anything happened to me on account of tonight, it would be just too bad for you. *You'd* be haunted, really. It's a bad rule that doesn't work two ways."

The woman looked at her husband. "He's right, John," she said tremulously. "We'd better let Lyons go."

The man nodded. He looked worried.

He spoke very stiffly to Marvin. "I don't agree entirely with all you've said," he pointed out, "but I admit that in order to protect you we'll have to let Lyons go. If you'll give me a hand we'll carry him out and put him in his car."

"Actually, I suppose, I'll be doing all the work."

"Yes," the man agreed, "you will."

They went into the little hall, and there, to Marvin's complete astonishment, crumpled on the floor lay old Lyons. Marvin recognized him easily from the newspaper photographs he had seen.

"Hard-looking duffer, isn't he?" Marvin said, trying to stifle a tremor in his voice.

The man nodded without speaking.

Together, Marvin watching the man narrowly, they carried the lax body out through the rain and put it into the big sedan. When the job was done the man stood silently for a moment, looking up into the black invisible clouds.

"It's clearing," he said matter-of-factly. "In an hour it'll be over."

"My wife'll kill me when I get home," Marvin said.

The man made a little clucking sound. "Maybe if you wiped your ignition now your car'd start. It's had a chance to dry a little."

"I'll try it," Marvin said. He opened the hood and wiped the distributor cap and points and around the spark plugs with his handkerchief. He got in the car and stepped on the starter, and the motor caught almost immediately.

The man stepped toward the door, and Marvin doubled his right fist, ready for anything. But then the man stopped.

"Well, I suppose you'd better be going along," he said. "Good night."

"Good night," Marvin said. "And thanks. I'll stop by one of these days and say hello."

"You wouldn't find us in," the man said simply.

By Heaven, he *is* nuts, Marvin thought. "Listen, brother," he said earnestly, "you aren't going to do anything funny to old Lyons after I'm gone?"

The other shook his head. "No. Don't worry."

Marvin let in the clutch and stepped on the gas. He wanted to get out of there as quickly as possible.

In Little Rock Falls he went into an all-night lunch and telephoned the police that there was an unconscious man sitting in a car three or four miles back on the detour. Then he drove home.

Early the next morning, on his way to work, he drove back over the detour.

He kept watching for the little house, and when it came in sight he recognized it easily from the contour of the rooms and the spacing of the windows and the little overhang above the door.

But as he came closer he saw that it was deserted. The windows were out, the steps had fallen in. The clapboards were gray and weather-beaten, and naked rafters showed through holes in the roof.

Marvin stopped his car and sat there beside the road for a little while, his face oddly pale. Finally he got out of the car and walked over to the house and went inside.

There was not one single stick of furniture in the rooms. Jagged scars showed in the ceilings where the electric fixtures had been torn away. The house had been wrecked years before by vandals, by neglect, by the merciless wearing of the sun and rain.

In shape alone were the hallway and living-room as Marvin remembered them. *"There,"* he thought, "is where the bookcases were. The table was *there*—the davenport *there*."

Suddenly he stooped, and stared at the dusty boards and underfoot.

On the naked floor lay the butt of a cigarette. And, a half dozen feet away, lay another cigarette that had not been smoked—that had not even been lighted!

Marvin turned around blindly, and, like an automaton, walked out of that house.

Three days later he read in the newspapers that Lieutenant-Governor Lyons was dead. The Lieutenant-Governor had collapsed, the item continued, while driving his own car home from the state capital the night the Felders bridge was washed out. The death was attributed to heart disease. . . .

After all, Lyons was not a young man.

So Marvin Phelps knew that, even though his considerate ghostly hosts had voluntarily relinquished their vengeance, blind, impartial nature had meted out justice. And, in a strange way, he felt glad that that was so, glad that Grace and John Reed had left to Fate the punishment they had planned to impose with their own ghostly hands. . . .

TO BE TAKEN WITH A GRAIN OF SALT

Charles Dickens

I have always noticed a prevalent want of courage, even among persons of superior intelligence and culture, as to imparting their own psychological experiences when those have been of a strange sort. Almost all men are afraid that what they could relate in such wise would find no parallel or response in a listener's internal life, and might be suspected or laughed at. A truthful traveller who should have seen some extraordinary creature in the likeness of a sea-serpent, would have no fear of mentioning it; but the same traveller having had some singular presentiment, impulse, vagary of thought, vision (so-called), dream, or other remarkable mental impression, would hesitate considerably before he would own to it. To this reticence I attribute much of the obscurity in which such subjects are involved. We do not habitually communicate our experiences of these subjective things, as we do our experiences of objective creation. The consequence is, that the general stock of experience in this regard appears exceptional, and really is so, in respect of being miserably imperfect.

In what I am going to relate I have no intention of setting up, opposing, or supporting, any theory whatever. I know the history of the Bookseller of Berlin, I have studied the case of the wife of a late Astronomer Royal as related by Sir David Brewster, and I have followed the minutest details of a much more remarkable case of Spectral Illusion occurring within my private circle of friends. It may be necessary to state as to this last that the sufferer (a lady) was in no degree, however distant, related to me. A mistaken assumption on that head, might suggest an explanation of a part of my own case—but only a part—which would be wholly without foundation. It cannot be referred to my inheritance of any developed peculiarity, nor had I ever before any at all similar experience, nor have I ever had any at all similar experience since.

It does not signify how many years ago, or how few, a certain Murder was committed in England, which attracted great attention. We hear more than enough of Murderers as they rise in succession to their atrocious eminence, and I would bury the memory of this particular brute, if I could, as his body was buried, in Newgate Jail. I purposely abstain from giving any direct clue to the criminal's individuality.

When the murder was first discovered, no suspicion fell—or I ought rather to say, for I cannot be too precise in my facts, it was nowhere publicly hinted that any suspicion fell—on the man who was afterwards brought to trial. As no reference was at that time made to him in the newspapers, it is obviously impossible that any description of him can at that time have been given in the newspapers. It is essential that this fact be remembered.

Unfolding at breakfast my morning paper, containing the account of that first discovery, I found it to be deeply interesting, and I read it with close attention. I read it twice, if not three times. The discovery had been made in a bedroom, and, when I laid down the paper, I was aware of a flash—rush—flow—I do not know what to call it—no word I can find is satisfactorily descriptive—in which I seemed to see that bedroom passing through my room, like a picture impossibly painted on a running river. Though almost instantaneous in its passing, it was perfectly clear; so clear that I distinctly, and with a sense of relief, observed the absence of the dead body from the bed.

It was in no romantic place that I had this curious sensation, but in chambers in Piccadilly, very near the corner of Saint James's Street. It was entirely new to me. I was in my easy-chair at the moment, and the sensation was accompanied with a peculiar shiver which started the chair from its position. (But it is to be noted that the chair ran easily on castors.) I went to one of the windows (there are two in the room, and the room is on the second floor) to refresh my eyes with the moving objects down in Piccadilly. It was a bright autumn morning, and the street was sparkling and cheerful. The wind was high. As I looked out, it brought down from the Park a quantity of fallen leaves, which a gust took, and whirled into a spiral pillar. As the pillar fell and the leaves dispersed, I saw two men on the opposite side of the way, going from West to East. They were one behind the other. The foremost man often looked back over his shoulder. The second man followed him, at a distance of some thirty paces, with his right hand menacingly raised. First, the singularity and steadiness of this threatening gesture in so public a thoroughfare, attracted my attention; and next, the more remarkable circumstance that nobody heeded it. Both men threaded their way among the other passengers, with a smoothness hardly consistent even with the action of walking on a pavement, and no single creature that I could see, gave them place, touched them, or looked after them. In passing before my windows, they both stared up at me. I saw their two faces very distinctly, and I knew that I could recognize them anywhere. Not that I had consciously noticed anything very remarkable in either face, except that the man who went first had an unusually lowering appearance, and that the face of the man who followed him was of the colour of impure wax.

I am a bachelor, and my valet and his wife constitute my whole establishment. My occupation is in a certain Branch Bank, and I wish that my duties as head of a Department were as light as they are popularly supposed to be. They kept me in town that autumn, when I stood in need of a change. I was not ill, but I was not well. My reader is to make the most that can be reasonably made of my feeling jaded, having a depressing sense upon me of a monotonous life, and being 'slightly dyspeptic.' I am assured by my renowned doctor that my real state of health at that time justifies no stronger description, and I quote his own from his written answer to my request for it.

As the circumstances of the Murder, gradually unravelling, took stronger and stronger possession of the public mind, I kept them away from mine, by knowing as little about them as was possible in the midst of the universal excitement. But I knew that a verdict of Willful Murder had been found against the suspected Murderer, and that he had been committed to Newgate for trial. I also knew that his trial had been postponed over one Sessions of the Central Criminal Court, on the ground of general prejudice and want of time for the preparation of the defence. I may further have known, but I believe I did not, when, or about when, the Sessions to which his trial stood postponed would come on.

My sitting-room, bedroom, and dressing-room, are all on one floor. With the last, there is no communication but through the bedroom. True, there is a door in it, once communicating with the staircase; but a part of the fitting of my bath has been—and had then been for some years—fixed across it. At the same period, and as a part of the same arrangement, the door had been nailed up and canvassed over.

I was standing in my bedroom late one night, giving some directions to my servant before he went to bed. My face was towards the only available door of communication with the dressing-room, and it was closed. My servant's back was towards that door. While I was speaking to him I saw it open, and a man look in, who very earnestly and mysteriously beckoned to me. That man was the man who had gone second of the two along Piccadilly, and whose face was the colour of impure wax.

The figure, having beckoned, drew back and closed the door. With no longer pause than was made by my crossing the bed-room, I opened the dressing-room door, and looked in. I had a lighted candle already in my hand. I felt no inward expectation of seeing the figure in the dressing-room, and I did not see it there.

Conscious that my servant stood amazed, I turned round to him, and said: 'Derrick, could you believe that in my cool senses I fancied I saw a——' As I there laid my hand upon his breast, with a sudden start he trembled violently, and said, 'O Lord yes sir! A dead man beckoning!'

Now, I do not believe that this John Derrick, my trusty and attached servant for more than twenty years, had any impression whatever of having seen any such figure, until I touched him. The change in him was so startling when I touched him, that I fully believe he derived his impression in some occult manner from me at that instant.

I bade John Derrick bring some brandy, and I gave him a dram, and was glad to take one myself. Of what had proceeded that night's phenomenon, I told him not a single word. Reflecting on it, I was absolutely certain that I had never seen that face before, except on the one occasion in Piccadilly. Comparing its expression when beckoning at the door, with its expression when it had stared up at me as I stood at my window, I came to the con-clusion that on the first occasion it had sought to fasten itself upon my memory, and that on the second occasion it had made sure of being immediately remembered.

I was not very comfortable that night, though I felt a certainty, difficult to explain, that the figure would not return. At daylight, I fell into a heavy sleep, from which I was awakened by John Derrick's coming to my bedside with a paper in his hand.

This paper, it appeared, had been the subject of an altercation at the door between its bearer and my servant. It was a summons to me to serve upon a Jury at the forthcoming Sessions of the Central Criminal Jury, as John Derrick well knew. He believed—I am not certain at this hour whether with reason or otherwise—that the class of Jurors were customarily chosen on a lower qualification than mine, and he had at first refused to accept the summons. The man who served it had taken the matter very coolly. He had said that my attendance or non-attendance was nothing to him; there the summons was; and I should deal with it at my own peril, and not at his.

For a day or two I was undecided whether to respond to this call, or take no notice of it. I was not conscious of the slightest mysterious bias, influence, or attraction, one way or other. Of that I am as strictly sure as of every other statement that I make here. Ultimately I decided, as a break in the monotony of my life, that I would go.

The appointed morning was a raw morning in the month of November. There was a dense brown fog in Piccadilly, and it became positively black and in the last degree oppressive East of Temple Bar. I found the passages and staircases of the Court House flaringly lighted with gas, and the Court itself similarly illuminated. I *think* that until I was conducted by officers into the Old Court and saw its crowded state, I did not know that the Murderer was to be tried that day. I *think* that until I was so helped into the Old Court with considerable difficulty, I did not know into which of the two Courts sitting, my summons would take me. But this must not be received as a positive assertion, for I am not completely satisfied in my mind on either point.

I took my seat in the place appropriated to Jurors in waiting, and I looked about the Court as well as I could through the cloud of fog and breath that was heavy in it. I noticed the black vapour hanging like a murky curtain outside the great windows, and I noticed the stifled sound of wheels on the straw or tan that was littered in the street; also, the hum of people gathered there, which a shrill whistle, or a louder song or hail than the rest, occasionally pierced. Soon afterwards the Judges, two in number, entered and took their seats. The buzz in the Court was awfully hushed. The direction was given to put the Murderer to the bar. He appeared there. And in that same instant I recognized in him, the first of the two men who had gone down Piccadilly.

If my name had been called then, I doubt if I could have answered to it audibly. But it was called about sixth or eighth in the panel, and I was by that time able to say 'Here!' Now, observe. As I stepped into the box, the prisoner, who had been looking on attentively but with no sign of concern, became violently agitated, and beckoned to his attorney. The prisoner's wish to challenge me was so manifest, that it occasioned a pause, during which the attorney, with his hand upon the dock, whispered to his client, and shook his head. I afterwards had it from that gentlemen, that the prisoner's first affrighted words to him were, '*At all hazards challenge that man!*' But, that as he would give no reason for it, and admitted that he had not even known my name until he heard it called and I appeared, it was not done.

Both on the ground already explained, that I wish to avoid reviving the unwholesome memory of that Murderer, and also because a detailed account of his long trial is by no means indispensable to my narrative, I shall confine myself closely to such incidents in the ten days and nights during which we, the Jury, were kept together, as directly bear on my own curious personal experience. It is in that, and not in the Murderer, that I seek to interest my reader. It is to that, and not to a page of the Newgate Calendar, that I beg attention.

I was chosen Foreman of the Jury. On the second morning of the trial, after evidence had been taken for two hours (I heard the church clocks strike), happening to cast my eyes over my brother-jurymen, I found an inexplicable difficulty in counting them. I counted them several times, yet always with the same difficulty. In short, I made them one too many.

I touched the brother-juryman whose place was next to me, and I whispered to him, 'Oblige me by counting us.' He looked surprised by the request, but turned his head and counted. 'Why,' says he, suddenly, 'We are Thirt——; but no, it's not possible. No. We are twelve.'

According to my counting that day, we were always right in detail, but in the gross we were always one too many. There was no appearance—no figure—to account for it; but I had now an inward foreshadowing of the figure that was surely coming.

The Jury were housed at the London Tavern. We all slept in one large room on separate tables, and we were constantly in the charge and under the eye of the officer sworn to hold us in safe-keeping. I see no reason for suppressing the real name of that officer. He was intelligent, highly polite, and obliging, and (I was glad to hear) much respected in the City. He had an agreeable presence, good eyes, enviable black whiskers, and a fine sonorous voice. His name was Mr Harker.

When we turned into our twelve beds at night, Mr Harker's bed was drawn across the door. On the night of the second day, not being disposed to lie down, and seeing Mr Harker sitting on his bed, I went and sat beside him, and offered him a pinch of snuff. As Mr Harker's hand touched mine in taking it from my box, a peculiar shiver crossed him, and he said: 'Who is this!'

Following Mr Harker's eyes and looking along the room, I saw again the figure I expected—the second of the two men who had gone down Piccadilly. I rose, and advanced a few steps; then stopped, and looked round at Mr Harker. He was quite unconcerned, laughed, and said in a pleasant way, 'I thought for a moment we had a thirteenth juryman, without a bed. But I see it is the moonlight.'

Making no revelation to Mr Harker, but inviting him to take a walk with me to the end of the room, I watched what the figure did. It stood for a few moments by the bedside of each of my eleven brother-jurymen, close to the pillow. It always went to the right-hand side of the bed, and always passed out crossing the foot of the next bed. It seemed from the action of the head, merely to look down pensively at each recumbent figure. It took no notice of me, or of my bed, which was that nearest to Mr Harker's. It seemed to go out where the moonlight came in, through a high window, as by an aerial flight of stairs.

Next morning at breakfast, it appeared that everybody present had dreamed of the murdered man last night, except myself and Mr Harker.

I now felt as convinced that the second man who had gone down Piccadilly was the murdered man (so to speak), as if it had been borne into my comprehension by his immediate testimony. But even this took place, and in a manner for which I was not at all prepared.

On the fifth day of the trial, when the case for the prosecution was drawing to a close, a miniature of the murdered man, missing from his bedroom upon the discovery of the deed, and afterwards found in a hiding-place where the Murderer had been seen digging, was put in evidence. Having been identified by the witness under examination, it was handed up to the Bench, and thence handed down to be inspected by the Jury. As an officer in a black gown was making his way with it across to me, the figure of the second man who had gone down Piccadilly, impetuously started from the crowd, caught the miniature from the officer, and gave it to me with its own hands, at the same time saying in a low and hollow tone—before I saw the miniature, which was in a locket—'*I was younger then, and my face was not then drained of blood.*' It also came between me and the brother-juryman to whom I would have given the miniature, and between him and the brother-juryman to whom he would have given it, and so passed it on through the whole of our number, and back into my possession. Not one of them, however, detected this.

At table, and generally when we were shut up together in Mr Harker's custody, we had from the first naturally discussed the days' proceedings a good deal. On that fifth day, the case for the prosecution being closed, and we having that side of the question in a completed shape before us, our discussion was more animated and serious. Among our number was a vestryman—the densest idiot I have ever seen at large—who met the plainest evidence with the most preposterous objections, and who was sided by two flabby parochial parasites; all the three empanelled from a district so delivered over to Fever that they ought to have been upon their own trial, for five hundred Murders. When these mischievous blockheads were at their loudest, which was towards midnight while some of us were already preparing for bed, I again saw the murdered man. He stood grimly behind them, beckoning to me. On my going towards them and striking into the conversation, he immediately retired. This was the beginning of a separate series of appearances, confined to that long room in which *we* were confined. Whenever a knot of my brother jurymen laid their heads together, I saw the head of the murdered man among theirs.

Whenever their comparison of notes was going against him, he would solemnly and irresistibly beckon to me.

It will be borne in mind that down to the production of the miniature on the fifth day of the trial, I had never seen the Appearance in Court. Three changes occurred, now that we entered on the case for the defence. Two of them I will mention together, first. The figure was now in Court continually, and it never there addressed itself to me, but always to the person who was speaking at the time. For instance. The throat of the murdered man had been cut straight across. In the opening speech for the defence, it was suggested that the deceased might have cut his own throat. At that very moment, the figure with its throat in the dreadful condition referred to (this it had concealed before) stood at the speaker's elbow, motioning across and across its windpipe, now with the right hand, now with the left, vigorously suggesting to the speaker himself, the impossibility of such a wound having been self-inflicted by either hand. For another instance. A witness to character, a woman, deposed to the prisoner's being the most amiable of mankind. The figure at that instant stood on the floor before her, looking her full in the face, and pointing out the prisoner's evil countenance with an extended arm and an outstretched finger.

The third change now to be added, impressed me strongly, as the most marked and striking of all. I do not theorize upon it; I accurately state it, and there leave it. Although the Appearance was not itself perceived by those whom it addressed, its coming close to such persons was invariably attended by some trepidation or disturbance on their part. It seemed to me as if it were prevented by laws to which I was not amenable, from fully revealing itself to others, and yet as if it could, invisibly, dumbly and darkly, overshadow their minds. When the leading counsel for the defence suggested that hypothesis of suicide and the figure stood at the learned gentleman's elbow, frightfully sawing at its severed throat, it is undeniable that the counsel faltered in his speech, lost for a few seconds the thread of his ingenious discourse, wiped his forehead with his handkerchief, and turned extremely pale. When the witness to character was confronted by the Appearance, her eyes most certainly did follow the direction of its pointed finger, and rest in great hesitation and trouble upon the prisoner's face. Two additional illustrations will suffice. On the eighth day of the trial, after the pause which was every day made early in the afternoon for a few minutes' rest and refreshment, I came back into Court with the rest of the Jury, some little time before the return of the Judges. Standing up in the box and looking about me, I thought the figure was not there, until, chancing to raise my eyes to the gallery, I saw it bending forward and leaning over a very decent woman, as if to assure itself whether the Judges had resumed their seats or not. Immediately afterwards, that woman screamed, fainted, and was carried out. So with the venerable, sagacious, and patient Judge who conducted the trial. When the case was over, and he settled himself and his papers to sum up, the murdered man entering by the Judges' door, advanced to his Lordship's desk, and looked eagerly over his shoulder at the pages of his notes which he was turning. A change came over his Lordship's face; his hand stopped; the peculiar shiver that I knew so well, passed over him; he faltered, 'Excuse me gentlemen, for a few moments. I am somewhat oppressed by the vitiated air;' and did not recover until he had drunk a glass of water.

Through all the monotony of six of those interminable ten days—the same Judges and others on the bench, the same Murderer in the dock, the same lawyers at the table, the same tones of question and answer rising to the roof of the court, the same scratching of the Judge's pen, the same ushers going in and out, the same lights kindled at the same hour when there had been any natural light of day, the same foggy curtain outside the great windows when it was foggy, the same rain pattering and dripping when it was rainy, the same footmarks of turnkeys and prisoner day after day on the same sawdust, the same keys locking and unlocking the same heavy doors—through all the wearisome monotony which made me feel as if I had been Foreman of the Jury for a vast period of time, and Piccadilly had flourished coevally with Babylon, the murdered man never lost one trace of his distinctness in my eyes, nor was he at any moment less distinct than anybody else. I must not omit, as a matter of fact, that I never once saw the Appearance which I call by the name of the murdered man, look at the Murderer. Again and again I wondered, 'Why does he not?' But he never did.

Nor did he look at me, after the production of the miniature, until the last closing minutes of the trial arrived. We retired to consider, at seven minutes before ten at night. The idiotic vestryman and his two parochial parasites gave us so much trouble, that we twice returned into Court, to beg to have certain extracts from the Judge's notes reread. Nine of us had not the smallest doubt about those passages, neither, I believe, had any one in Court; the dunder-headed triumvirate however, having no idea but obstruction, disputed them for that very reason. At length we prevailed, and finally the Jury returned into Court at ten minutes past twelve.

The murdered man at that time stood directly opposite the Jury-box, on the other side of the Court. As I took my place, his eyes rested on me, with great attention; he seemed satisfied, and slowly shook a great grey veil, which he carried on his arm for the first time, over his head and whole form. As I gave in our verdict 'Guilty', the veil collapsed, all was gone, and his place was empty.

The Murderer being asked by the Judge, according to usage, whether he had anything to say before sentence of Death should be passed upon him, indistinctly muttered something which was described in the leading newspapers of the following day as 'a few rambling, incoherent, and half-audible words, in which he was understood to complain that he had not had a fair trial because the Foreman of the Jury was prepossessed against him.' The remarkable declaration that he really made, was this: *'My Lord, I knew I was a doomed man when the Foreman of my Jury came into the box. My Lord, I knew he would never let me off, because, before I was taken, he somehow got to my bedside in the night, woke me, and put a rope round my neck.'*

ACROSS THE MOORS

William Fryer Harvey

It really was most unfortunate.

Peggy had a temperature of nearly a hundred, and a pain in her side, and Mrs. Workington Bancroft knew that it was appendicitis. But there was no one whom she could send for the doctor.

James had gone with the jaunting-car to meet her husband, who had at last managed to get away for a week's shooting.

Adolph, she had sent to the Evershams, only half an hour before, with a note for Lady Eva.

The cook could not manage to walk, even if dinner could be served without her.

Kate, as usual, was not to be trusted.

There remained Miss Craig.

"Of course, you must see that Peggy is really ill," said she, as the governess came into the room, in answer to her summons. "The difficulty is, that there is absolutely no one whom I can send for the doctor." Mrs. Workington Bancroft paused; she was always willing that those beneath her should have the privilege of offering the services which it was her right to command.

"So, perhaps, Miss Craig," she went on, "you would not mind walking over to Tebbits' Farm. I hear there is a Liverpool doctor staying there. Of course I know nothing about him, but we must take the risk, and I expect he'll be only too glad to be earning something during his holiday. It's nearly four miles, I know, and I'd never dream of asking you if it was not that I dread appendicitis so."

"Very well," said Miss Craig, "I suppose I must go; but I don't know the way."

"Oh you can't miss it," said Mrs. Workington Bancroft, in her anxiety temporarily forgiving the obvious unwillingness of her governess' consent.

"You follow the road across the moor for two miles, until you come to Redman's Cross. You turn to the left there, and follow a rough path that leads through a larch plantation. The Tebbits' farm lies just below you in the valley."

"And take Pontiff with you," she added, as the girl left the room. "There's absolutely nothing to be afraid of, but I expect you'll feel happier with the dog."

"Well, miss," said the cook, when Miss Craig went into the kitchen to get her boots, which had been drying by the fire; "of course she knows best, but I don't think it's right after all that's happened for the mistress to send you across the moors on a night like this. It's not as if the doctor could do anything for Miss Margaret if you do bring him. Every child is like that once in a while. He'll only say put her to bed, and she's there already."

"I don't see what there is to be afraid of, cook," said Miss Craig as she laced her boots, "unless you believe in ghosts."

"I'm not so sure about that. Anyhow I don't like sleeping in a bed where the sheets are too short for you to pull them over your head. But don't you be frightened, miss, It's my belief that their bark is worse than their bite."

But though Miss Craig amused herself for some minutes by trying to imagine the bark of a ghost (a thing altogether different from the classical ghostly bark), she did not feel entirely at her ease.

She was naturally nervous, and living as she did in the hinterland of the servants' hall, she had heard vague details of true stories that were only myths in the drawing room.

The very name of Redman's Cross sent a shiver through her; it must have been the place where that horrid murder was committed. She had forgotten the tale, though she remembered the name.

Her first disaster came soon enough.

Pontiff, who was naturally slow-witted, took more than five minutes to find out that it was only the governess he was escorting, but once the discovery had been made, he promptly turned tail, paying not the slightest heed to Miss Craig's feeble whistle. And then, to add to her discomfort, the rain came, not in heavy drops, but driving in sheets of thin spray that blotted out what few landmarks there were upon the moor.

They were very kind at Tebbits' farm. The doctor had gone back to Liverpool the day before, but Mrs. Tebbit gave her hot milk and turf cakes, and offered her reluctant son to show Miss Craig a shorter path on the moor, that avoided the larch wood.

He was a monosyllabic youth, but his presence was cheering, and she felt the night doubly black when he left her at the last gate.

She trudged on wearily. Her thoughts had already gone back to the almost exhausted theme of the bark of ghosts, when she heard steps on the road behind her that were at least material. Next minute the figure of a man appeared: Miss Craig was relieved to see that the stranger was a clergyman. He raised his hat. "I believe we are both going in the same direction," he said.

"Perhaps I may have the pleasure of escorting you." She thanked him. "It is rather weird at night," she went on, "and what with all the tales of ghosts and bogies that one hears from the country people, I've ended by being half afraid myself."

"I can understand your nervousness," he said, "especially on a night like this. I used at one time to feel the same, for my work often meant lonely walks across the moor to farms which were only reached by rough tracks difficult enough to find even in the daytime."

"And you never saw anything to frighten you—nothing immaterial I mean?"

"I can't really say that I did, but I had an experience eleven years ago which served as the turning point in my life, and since you seem to be now in much the same state of mind as I was then in, I will tell it you.

"The time of year was late September. I had been over to Westondale to see an old woman who was dying, and then, just as I was about to start on my way home, word came to me of another of my parishioners who had been suddenly taken ill only that morning. It was after seven when at last I started. A farmer saw me on my way, turning back when I reached the moor road.

"The sunset the previous evening had been one of the most lovely I ever remember seeing. The whole vault of heaven had been scattered with flakes of white cloud, tipped with rosy pink like the strewn petals of a full-blown rose.

"But that night all was changed. The sky was an absolutely dull slate colour, except in one corner of the west where a thin rift showed the last saffron tint of the sullen sunset. As I walked, stiff and footsore, my spirits sank. It must have been the marked contrast between the two evenings, the one so lovely, so full of promise (the corn was still out in the fields spoiling for fine weather), the other so gloomy, so sad with all the dead weight of autumn and winter days to come. And then added to this sense of heavy depression came another different feeling which I surprised myself by recognising as fear.

"I did not know why I was afraid.

"The moors lay on either side of me, unbroken except for a straggling line of turf shooting butts, that stood within a stone's-throw of the road.

"The only sound I had heard for the last half hour was the cry of the startled grouse—Go back, go back, go back. But yet the feeling of fear was there, affecting a low centre of my brain through some little used physical channel.

"I buttoned my coat closer, and tried to divert my thoughts by thinking of next Sunday's sermon.

"I had chosen to preach on Job. There is much in the old-fashioned notion of the book, apart from all the subtleties of the higher criticism, that appeals to country people; the loss of herd and crops, the break up of the family. I would not have dared to speak, had not I too been a farmer; my own glebe land had been flooded three weeks before, and I suppose I stood to lose as much as any man in the parish. As I walked along the road repeating to myself the first chapter of the book, I stopped at the twelfth verse.

" 'And the Lord said unto Satan: Behold all that he hath is in thy power'. . .

"The thought of the bad harvest (and that is an awful thought in these valleys) vanished. I seemed to gaze into an ocean of infinite darkness.

"I had often used, with the Sunday glibness of the tired priest, whose duty it is to preach three sermons in one day, the old simile of the chess-board. God and the Devil were the players: and we were helping one side or the other. But until that night had not thought of the possibility of my being only a pawn in the game, that God might throw away that the game might be won.

"I had reached the place where we are now, I remember it by that rough stone water-trough, when a man suddenly jumped up from the roadside. He had been seated on a heap of broken road metal.

" 'Which way are you going, guv'ner?' " he said.

"I knew from the way he spoke that the man was a stranger. There are many at this time of the year who come up from the south, tramping northwards with the ripening corn. I told him my destination.

" 'We'll go along together,' he replied.

"It was too dark to see much of the man's face, but what little I made out was coarse and brutal.

"Then he began the half-menacing whine I knew so well—he had tramped miles that day, he had had no food since breakfast and that was only a crust.

" 'Give us a copper,' he said, 'it's only for a night's lodging.'

"He was whittling away with a big clasp knife at an ash stake he had taken from some hedge."

The clergyman broke off.

"Are those the lights of your house?" he said. "We are nearer than I expected, but I shall have time to finish my story. I think I will, for you can run home in a couple of minutes, and I don't want you to be frightened when you are out on the moors again.

"As the man talked he seemed to have stepped out of the very background of my thoughts, his sordid tale, with the sad lies that hid a far sadder truth.

"He asked me the time.

"It was five minutes to nine. As I replaced my watch I glanced at his face. His teeth were clenched, and there was something in the gleam of his eyes that told me at once his purpose.

"Have you ever known how long a second is? For a third of a second I stood there facing him, filled with an overwhelming pity for myself and him; and then without a word of warning he was upon me. I felt nothing. A flash of lightning ran down my spine, I heard the dull crash of the ash stake, and then a very gentle patter like the sound of a far-distant stream. For a minute I lay in perfect happiness watching the lights of the house as they increased in number until the whole heaven shone with twinkling lamps.

"I could not have had a more painless death."

Miss Craig looked up. The man was gone; she was alone on the moor.

She ran to the house, her teeth chattering, ran to the solid shadow that crossed and recrossed the kitchen blind.

As she entered the hall, the clock on the stairs struck the hour. It was nine o'clock.

THE HALL BEDROOM

Mary E. Wilkins

My name is Mrs. Elizabeth Jennings. I am a highly respectable woman. I may style myself a gentlewoman, for in my youth I enjoyed advantages. I was well brought up, and I graduated at a young ladies' seminary. I also married well. My husband was that most genteel of all merchants, an apothecary. His shop was on the corner of the main street in Rockton, the town where I was born, and where I lived until the death of my husband. My parents had died when I had been married a short time, so I was left quite alone in the world. I was not competent to carry on the apothecary business by myself, for I had no knowledge of drugs, and had a mortal terror of giving poisons instead of medicines. Therefore I was obliged to sell at a considerable sacrifice, and the proceeds, some five thousand dollars, were all I had in the world. The income was not enough to support me in any kind of comfort, and I saw that I must in some way earn money. I thought at first of teaching, but I was no longer young, and methods had changed since my school days. What I was able to teach, nobody wished to know. I could think of only one thing to do: take boarders. But the same objection to that business as to teaching held good in Rockton. Nobody wished to board. My husband had rented a house with a number of bedrooms, and I advertised, but nobody applied. Finally my cash was running very low, and I became desperate. I packed my furniture, rented a large house in this town, and moved there. It was a venture attended with many risks. In the first place the rent was exorbitant; in the next I was entirely unknown. However, I am a person of considerable ingenuity, and have inventive power, and much enterprise when the occasion presses. I advertised in a very original manner, although that actually took my last penny, that is, the last penny of my ready money, and I was forced to draw on my principal to purchase my first supplies, a thing which I had resolved never on any account to do. But the great risk met with a reward, for I had several applicants within two days after my advertisement appeared in the paper. Within two weeks my boarding-house was well established, I became very successful, and my success would have been uninterrupted had it not been for the mysterious and bewildering occurrences which I am about to relate. I am now forced to leave the house and rent another. Some of my old boarders accompany me, some, with the most unreasonable nervousness, refuse to be longer associated in any way, however indirectly, with the terrible and uncanny happening which I have to relate. It remains to be seen whether my ill luck in this house will follow me into another, and whether my whole prosperity in life will be forever shadowed by the Mystery of the Hall Bedroom. Instead of telling the strange story myself in my own words, I shall present the Journal of Mr. George H. Wheatcroft. I shall show you the portions beginning on January 18 of the present year, the date when he took up his residence with me. Here it is:

"*January 18, 1883.* Here I am established in my new boarding-house. I have, as befits my humble means, the hall bedroom, even the hall bedroom on the third floor. I have heard all of my life of hall bedrooms, I have seen hall bedrooms, I have been in them, but never until now, when I am actually established in one, did I comprehend what, at once, an ignominious and sternly uncompromising thing a hall bedroom is. It proves the ignominy of the dweller therein. No man at thirty-six (my age) would be domiciled in a hall bedroom unless he were himself ignominious, as least comparatively speaking. I am proved by this means incontrovertibly to have been left far behind in the race. I see no reason why I should not live in this hall bedroom for the rest of my life, that is, if I have money enough to pay the landlady, and that seems probable, since my small funds are invested as safely as if I were an orphan-ward in charge of a pillar of a sanctuary. After the valuables have been stolen, I have most carefully locked the stable door. I have experienced the revulsion which comes sooner or later to the adventurous soul who experiences nothing but defeat and so-called ill luck. I have swung to the opposite extreme. I have lost in everything—I have lost in love, I have lost in money, I have lost in the struggle for preferment, I have lost in health and strength. I am now settled down in a hall bedroom to live upon my small income, and regain my health by mild potations of the mineral waters here, if possible; if not, to live here without my health—for mine is not a necessarily fatal malady—until Providence shall take me out of my hall bedroom. There is no one place more than another where I care to live. There is not sufficient motive to take me away, even if the mineral waters do not benefit me. So I am here and to stay in the hall bedroom. The landlady is civil, and even kind, as kind as a woman who has to keep her poor womanly eye upon the main chance can be. The struggle for money always injures the fine grain of a woman; she is too fine a thing to do it; she does not by nature belong with the gold grubbers, and it therefore lowers her; she steps from heights to claw and scrape and dig. But she cannot help it oftentimes, poor thing, and her deterioration hereby is to be condoned. The landlady is all she can be, taking her strain of adverse circumstances into consideration, and the table is good, even conscientiously so. It looks to me as if she were foolish enough to strive to give the boarders their money's worth, with the due regard for the main chance which is inevitable. However, that is of minor importance to me, since my diet is restricted.

"It is curious what an annoyance a restriction in diet can be even to a man who has considered himself somewhat indifferent to gastronomic delights. There was to-day a pudding for dinner, which I could not taste without penalty, but which I longed for. It was only because it looked unlike any other pudding that I had ever seen, and assumed a mental and spiritual significance. It seemed to me, whimsically no doubt, as if tasting it might give me a new sensation, and consequently a new outlook. Trivial things may lead to large results: why should I not get a new outlook by means of a pudding? Life here stretches before me most monotonously, and I feel like clutching at alleviations, though paradoxically, since I have settled down with the utmost acquiescence. Still, one cannot immediately overcome and change radically all one's nature. Now I look at myself critically and search for the keynote to my whole self, and my actions, I have always been conscious of a reaching out, an overweening desire for the new, the untried, for the broadness of further horizons, the seas beyond seas, the thought beyond thought. This characteristic has been the primary cause of all my misfortunes. I have the soul of an explorer, and in nine out of ten cases this leads to destruction. If I had possessed capital and sufficient push, I should have been one of the searchers after the North Pole. I have been an eager student of astronomy. I have studied botany with avidity, and have dreamed of new flora in unexplored parts of the world, and the same with animal life and geology. I longed for riches in order to discover the power and sense of possession of the rich. I longed for love in order to discover the possibilities of the emotions. I longed for all that the mind of man could conceive as desirable for man, not so much for purely selfish ends, as from an insatiable thirst for knowledge of a universal trend. But I have limitations, I do not quite understand of what nature—for what mortal ever did quite understand his own limitations, since a knowledge of them would preclude their existence?—but they have prevented my progress to any extent. Therefore behold me in my hall bedroom, settled at last into a groove of fate so deep that I have lost the sight of even my horizons. Just at present, as I write here, my horizon on the left, that is my physical horizon, is a wall covered with cheap paper. The paper is an indeterminate pattern in white and gilt. There are a few photographs of my own hung about, and on the large wall space beside the bed there is a large oil painting which belongs to my landlady. It has a massive tarnished gold frame, and, curiously enough, the painting itself is rather good. I have no idea who the artist could have been. It is of the conventional landscape type in vogue some fifty years since, the type so fondly reproduced in chromos—the winding river with the little boat occupied by a pair of lovers, the cottage nestled among trees on the right shore, the gentle slope of the hills and the church spire in the background—but still it is well done. It gives me the impression of an artist without the slightest originality of design, but much of technique. But for some inexplicable reason the picture frets me. I find myself gazing at it when I do not wish to do so. It seems to compel my attention like some intent face in the room. I shall ask Mrs. Jennings to have it removed. I will hang in its place some photographs which I have in a trunk.

"*January 26.* I do not write regularly in my journal. I never did. I see no reason why I should. I see no reason why anyone should have the slightest sense of duty in such a matter. Some days I have nothing which interests me sufficiently to write out, some days I feel either too ill or too indolent. For four days I have not written, from a mixture of all three reasons. Now, to-day I both feel like it and I have something to write. Also I am distinctly better than I have been. Perhaps the waters are benefiting me, or the change of air. Or possibly it is something else more subtle. Possibly my mind has seized upon something new, a discovery which causes it to react upon my failing body and serves as a stimulant. All I know is, I feel distinctly better, and am conscious of an acute interest in doing so, which is of late strange to me. I have been rather indifferent, and sometimes have wondered if that were not the cause rather than the result of my state of health. I have been so continually balked that I have settled into a state of inertia. I lean rather comfortably against my obstacles. After all, the worst of the pain always lies in the struggle. Give up and it is rather pleasant than otherwise. If one did not kick, the pricks would not in the least matter. However, for some reason, for the last few days, I seem to have awakened from my state of quiescence. It means future trouble for me, no doubt, but in the meantime I am not sorry. It began with the picture—the large oil painting. I went to Mrs. Jennings about it yesterday, and she, to my surprise—for I thought it a matter that could be easily arranged—objected to having it removed. Her reasons were two; both simple, both sufficient, especially since I, after all, had no very strong desire either way. It seems that the picture does not belong to her. It hung here when she rented the house. She says, if it is removed, a very large and unsightly discoloration of the wall paper will be exposed, and she does not like to ask for new paper. The owner, an old man, is travelling abroad, the agent is curt, and she has only been in the house a very short time. Then it would mean a sad upheaval of my room, which would disturb me. She also says that there is no place in the house where she can store the picture, and there is not a vacant space in another room for one so large. So I let the picture remain. It really, when I came to think of it, was very immaterial after all. But I got my photographs out of my trunk, and I hung them around the large picture. The wall is almost completely covered. I hung them yesterday afternoon, and last night I repeated a strange experience which I have had in some degree every night since I have been here, but was not sure whether it deserved the name of experience, but was not rather one of those dreams in which one dreams one is awake. But last night it came again, and now I know. There is something very singular about this room. I am very much interested. I will write down for future reference the events of last night. Concerning those of the preceding nights since I have slept in this room, I will simply say that they have been of a similar nature, but, as it were, only the preliminary stages, the prologue to what happened last night.

"I am not depending upon the mineral waters here as the one remedy for my malady, which is sometimes of an acute nature, and indeed constantly threatens me with considerable suffering unless by medicine I can keep it in check. I will say that the medicine which I employ is not of the class commonly known as drugs. It is impossible that it can be held responsible for what I am about to transcribe. My mind last night and every night since I have slept in this room was in an absolutely normal state. I take this medicine, prescribed by the specialist whose charge I was in before coming here, regularly every four hours while awake. As I am never a good sleeper, it follows that I am enabled with no inconvenience to take any medicine during the night with the same regularity as during the day. It is my habit, therefore, to place my bottle and spoon where I can put my hand upon them easily without lighting the gas. Since I have been in this room, I have placed the bottle of medicine upon my dresser at the side of the room opposite the bed. I have done this rather than place it nearer, as once I jostled the bottle and spilled most of the contents, and it is not easy for me to replace it, as it is expensive. Therefore I placed it in security on the dresser, and, indeed, that is but three or four steps from my bed, the room being so small. Last night I wakened as usual, and I knew, since I had fallen asleep about eleven, that it must be in the neighbourhood of three. I wake with almost clock-like regularity, and it is never necessary for me to consult my watch.

"I had slept unusually well and without dreams, and I awoke fully at once, with a feeling of refreshment to which I am not accustomed. I immediately got out of bed and began stepping across the room in the direction of my dresser, on which I had set my medicine bottle and spoon.

"To my utter amazement, the steps which had hitherto sufficed to take me across my room did not suffice to do so. I advanced several paces, and my outstretched hands touched nothing. I stopped and went on again. I was sure that I was moving in a straight direction, and even if I had not been I knew it was impossible to advance in any direction in my tiny apartment without coming into collision either with a wall or a piece of furniture. I continued to walk falteringly, as I have seen people on the stage: a step, then a long falter, then a sliding step. I kept my hands extended; they touched nothing. I stopped again. I had not the least sentiment of fear or consternation. It was rather the very stupefaction of surprise. 'How is this?' seemed thundering in my ears. 'What is this?'

"The room was perfectly dark. There was nowhere any glimmer, as is usually the case, even in a so-called dark room, from the walls, picture-frames, looking-glass or white objects. It was absolute gloom. The house stood in a quiet part of the town. There were many trees about; the electric street lights were extinguished at midnight; there was no moon and the sky was cloudy. I could not distinguish my one window, which I thought strange, even on such a dark night. Finally I changed my plan of motion and turned, as nearly as I could estimate, at right angles. Now, I thought, I must reach soon, if I kept on, my writing-table underneath the window; or, if I am going in the opposite direction, the hall door. I reached neither. I am telling the unvarnished truth when I say that I began to count my steps and carefully measure my paces after that, and I traversed a space clear of furniture at least twenty feet by thirty—a very large apartment. And as I walked I was conscious that my naked feet were pressing something which gave rise to sensations the like of which I had never experienced before. As nearly as I can express it, it was as if my feet pressed something as elastic as air or water, which was in this case unyielding to my weight. It gave me a curious sensation of buoyancy and stimulation. At the same time this surface, if surface be the right name, which I trod, felt cool to my feet with the coolness of vapour or fluidity, seeming to overlap the soles. Finally I stood still; my surprise was at last merging into a measure of consternation. 'Where am I?' I thought. 'What am I going to do?' Stories that I had heard of travellers being taken from their beds and conveyed into strange and dangerous places, Middle Age stories of the Inquisition flashed through my brain. I knew all the time that for a man who had gone to bed in a commonplace hall bedroom in a very commonplace little town such surmises were highly ridiculous, but it is hard for the human mind to grasp anything but a human explanation of phenomena. Almost anything seemed then, and seems now, more rational than an explanation bordering upon the supernatural, as we understand the supernatural. At last I called, though rather softly, 'What does this mean?' I said quite aloud, 'Where am I? Who is here? Who is doing this? I tell you I will have no such nonsense. Speak, if there is anybody here.' But all was dead silence. Then suddenly light flashed through the open transom of my door. Somebody had heard me—a man who rooms next door, a decent kind of man, also here for his health. He turned on the gas in the hall and called to me. 'What's the matter?' he asked, in an agitated, trembling voice. He is a nervous fellow.

"Directly, when the light flashed through my transom, I saw that I was in my familiar hall bedroom. I could see everything quite distinctly—my tumbled bed, my writing-table, my dresser, my chair, my little washstand, my clothes hanging on a row of pegs, the old picture on the wall. The picture gleamed out with singular distinctness in the light from the transom. The river seemed actually to run and ripple, and the boat to be gliding with the current. I gazed fascinated at it, as I replied to the anxious voice:

" 'Nothing is the matter with me,' said I. 'Why?'

" 'I thought I heard you speak,' said the man outside. 'I thought maybe you were sick.'

" 'No,' I called back. "I am all right. I am trying to find my medicine in the dark, that's all. I can see now you have lighted the gas."

" 'Nothing is the matter?'

" 'No; sorry I disturbed you. Good-night.'

" 'Good-night.' Then I heard the man's door shut after a minute's pause. He was evidently not quite satisfied. I took a pull at my medicine bottle, and got into bed. He had left the hall gas burning. I did not go to sleep again for some time. Just before I did so, someone, probably Mrs. Jennings, came out in the hall and extinguished the gas. This morning when I awoke everything was as usual in my room. I wonder if I shall have any such experience to-night.

"*January 27.* I shall write in my journal every day until this draws to some definite issue. Last night my strange experience deepened, as something tells me it will continue to do. I retired quite early, at half-past ten. I took the precaution, on retiring, to place beside my bed, on a chair, a box of safety matches, that I might not be in the dilemma of the night before. I took my medicine on retiring; that made me due to wake at half-past two. I had not fallen asleep directly, but had had certainly three hours of sound, dreamless slumber when I awoke. I lay a few minutes hesitating whether or not to strike a safety match and light my way to the dresser, whereon stood my medicine bottle. I hesitated, not because I had the least sensation of fear, but because of the same shrinking from a nerve shock that leads one at times to dread the plunge into an icy bath. It seemed much easier to me to strike that match and cross my hall bedroom to my dresser, take my dose, then return quietly to my bed, than to risk the chance of floundering about in some unknown limbo either of fancy or reality.

"At last, however, the spirit of adventure, which has always been such a ruling one for me, conquered. I rose. I took the box of safety matches in my hand, and started on, as I conceived, the straight course for my dresser, about five feet across from my bed. As before, I travelled and travelled and did not reach it. I advanced with groping hands extended, setting one foot cautiously before the other, but I touched nothing except the indefinite, unnameable surface which my feet pressed. All of a sudden, though, I became aware of something. One of my senses was saluted, nay, more than that, hailed, with imperiousness, and that was, strangely enough, my sense of smell, but in a hitherto unknown fashion. It seemed as if the odour reached my mentality first. I reversed the usual process, which is, as I understand it, like this: the odour when encountered strikes first the olfactory nerve, which transmits the intelligence to the brain. It is as if, to put it rudely, my nose met a rose, and then the nerve belonging to the sense said to my brain, 'Here is a rose.' This time my brain said, 'Here is a rose,' and my sense then recognized it. I say rose, but it was not a rose, that is, not the fragrance of any rose which I had ever known. It was undoubtedly a flower odour, and rose came perhaps the nearest to it. My mind realized it first with what seemed a leap of rapture. 'What is this delight?' I asked myself. And then the ravishing fragrance smote my sense. I breathed it in and it seemed to feed my thoughts, satisfying some hitherto unknown hunger. Then I took a step further and another fragrance appeared, which I liken to lilies for lack of something better, and then came violets, then mignonette. I cannot describe the experience, but it was a sheer delight, a rapture of sublimated sense. I groped further and further, and always into new waves of fragrance. I seemed to be wading breast-high through flower beds of Paradise, but all the time I touched nothing with my groping hands. At last a sudden giddiness as of surfeit overcame me. I realized that I might be in some unknown peril. I was distinctly afraid. I struck one of my safety matches, and I was in my hall bedroom, midway between my bed and my dresser. I took my dose of medicine and went to bed, and after a while fell sleep and did not wake till morning.

"*January 28.* Last night I did not take my usual dose of medicine. In these days of new remedies and mysterious results upon certain organizations, it occurred to me to wonder if possibly the drug might have, after all, something to do with my strange experience.

"I did not take my medicine. I put the bottle as usual on my dresser, since I feared if I interrupted further the customary sequence of affairs I might fail to wake. I placed my box of matches on the chair beside the bed. I fell asleep about quarter past eleven o'clock, and I waked when the clock was striking two—a little earlier than my wont. I did not hesitate this time. I rose at once, took my box of matches and proceeded as formerly. I walked what seemed a great space without coming into collision with anything.

I kept sniffing for the wonderful fragrances of the night before, but they did not recur. Instead, I was suddenly aware that I was tasting something, some morsel of sweetness hitherto unknown, and, as in the case of the odour, the usual order seemed reversed, and it was as if I tasted it first in my mental consciousness. Then the sweetness rolled under my tongue. I thought involuntarily of 'Sweeter than honey or the honeycomb' of the Scripture. I thought of the Old Testament manna. An ineffable content as of satisfied hunger seized me. I stepped further, and a new savour was upon my palate. And so on. It was never cloying, though of such sharp sweetness that it fairly stung. It was the merging of a material sense into a spiritual one. I said to myself, 'I have lived my life and always have I gone hungry until now.' I could feel my brain act swiftly under the influence of this heavenly food as under a stimulant. Then suddenly I repeated the experience of the night before. I grew dizzy, and an indefinite fear and shrinking were upon me. I struck my safety match and was back in my hall bedroom. I returned to bed, and soon fell asleep. I did not take my medicine. I am resolved not to do so longer. I am feeling much better.

"*January 29.* Last night to bed as usual, matches in place; fell asleep about eleven and waked at half-past one. I heard the half-hour strike; I am waking earlier and earlier every night. I had not taken my medicine, though it was on the dresser as usual. I again took my match-box in hand and started to cross the room, and, as always, traversed strange spaces, but this night, as seems fated to be the case every night, my experience was different. Last night I neither smelled nor tasted, but I heard—my Lord, I heard! The first sound of which I was conscious was one like the constantly gathering and receding murmur of a river, and it seemed to come from the wall behind my bed where the old picture hangs. Nothing in nature except a river gives that impression of at once advance and retreat. I could not mistake it. On, ever on, came the swelling murmur of the waves; past and ever past they died in the distance. Then I heard above the murmur of the river a song in an unknown tongue which I recognized as being unknown, yet which I understood; but the understanding was in my brain, with no words of interpretation. The song had to do with me, but with me in unknown futures for which I had no images of comparison in the past; yet a sort of ecstasy as of a prophecy of bliss filled my whole consciousness. The song never ceased, but as I moved on I came into new sound waves. There was the pealing of bells which might have been made of crystal, and might have summoned to the gates of heaven. There was music of strange instruments, great harmonies pierced now and then by small whispers as of love, and it all filled me with a certainty of a future of bliss.

"At last I seemed the centre of a mighty orchestra which constantly deepened and increased until I seemed to feel myself being lifted gently but mightily upon the waves of sound as upon the waves of a sea. Then again the terror and the impulse to flee to my own familiar scenes were upon me. I struck my match and was back in my hall bedroom. I do not see how I sleep at all after such wonders, but sleep I do. I slept dreamlessly until daylight this morning.

"*January 30.* I heard yesterday something with regard to my hall bedroom which affected me strangely. I cannot for the life of me say whether it intimidated me, filled me with the horror of the abnormal, or rather roused to a greater degree my spirit of adventure and discovery. I was down at the Cure, and was sitting on the veranda sipping idly my mineral water, when somebody spoke my name. 'Mr. Wheatcroft?' said the voice politely, interrogatively, somewhat apologetically, as if to provide for a possible mistake in my identity. I turned and saw a gentleman whom I recognized at once. I seldom forget names or faces. He was a Mr. Addison whom I had seen considerable of three years ago at a little summer hotel in the mountains. It was one of those passing acquaintances which signify little one way or the other. If never renewed, you have no regret; if renewed, you accept the renewal with no hesitation. It is in every way negative. But just now, in my feeble, friendless state, the sight of a face which beams with pleased remembrance is rather gratifying. I felt distinctly glad to see the man. He sat down beside me. He also had a glass of the water. His health, while not as bad as mine, leaves much to be desired.

"Addison had often been in this town before. He had in fact lived here at one time. He had remained at the Cure three years, taking the waters daily. He therefore knows about all there is to be known about the town, which is not very large. He asked me where I was staying and when I told him the street, rather excitedly inquired the number. When I told him the number, which is 240, he gave a manifest start, and after one sharp glance at me sipped his water in silence for a moment. He had so evidently betrayed some ulterior knowledge with regard to my residence that I questioned him.

" 'What do you know about 240 Pleasant Street?' said I.

" 'Oh nothing,' he replied, evasively, sipping his water.

"After a little while, however, he inquired, in what he evidently tried to render a casual tone, what room I occupied. 'I once lived a few weeks at 240 Pleasant Street myself,' he said. 'That house always was a boarding-house, I guess.'

" 'It had stood vacant for a term of years before the present occupant rented it, I believe,' I remarked. Then I answered his question. 'I have the hall bedroom on the third floor,' said I. 'The quarters are pretty straitened, but comfortable enough as hall bedrooms go.'

"But Mr. Addison had showed such unmistakable consternation at my reply that then I persisted in my questioning as to the cause, and at last he yielded and told me what he knew. He had hesitated both because he shrank from displaying what I might consider an unmanly superstition, and because he did not wish to influence me beyond what the facts of the case warranted. 'Well, I will tell you, Wheatcroft,' he said. 'Briefly all I know is this: When last I heard of 240 Pleasant Street it was not rented because of foul play which was supposed to have taken place there, though nothing was ever proved. There were two disappearances, and—in each case—of an occupant of the hall bedroom which you now have. The first disappearance was of a very beautiful girl who had come here for her health and was said to be the victim of a profound melancholy, induced by a love disappointment. She obtained board at 240 and occupied the hall bedroom about two weeks; then one morning she was gone, having seemingly vanished into thin air. Her relatives were communicated with; she had not many, nor friends either, poor girl, and a thorough search was made, but the last I knew she had never come to light. There were two or three arrests, but nothing ever came of them. Well, that was before my day here, but the second disappearance took place when I was in the house—a fine young fellow who had overworked in college. He had to pay his own way. He had taken cold, had the grip, and that and the overwork about finished him, and he came on here for a month's rest and recuperation. He had been in that room about two weeks, a little less, when one morning he wasn't there. Then there was a great hullabaloo. It seems that he had let fall some hints to the effect that there was something queer about the room, but, of course, the police did not think much of that. They made arrests right and left, but they never found him, and the arrested were discharged, though some of them are probably under a cloud of suspicion to this day. Then the boarding-house was shut up. Six years ago nobody would have boarded there, much less occupied that hall bedroom, but now I suppose new people have come in, and the story has died out. I dare say your landlady will not thank me for reviving it.'

"I assured him that it would make no possible difference to me. He looked at me sharply, and asked bluntly if I had seen anything wrong or unusual about the room. I replied, guarding myself from falsehood with a quibble, that I had seen nothing in the least unusual about the room, as indeed I had not, and have not now, but that may come. I feel that that will come in due time. Last night I neither saw, nor heard, nor smelled, nor tasted, but I—felt. Last night, having started again on my exploration of, God knows what, I had not advanced a step before I touched something. My first sensation was one of disappointment. 'It is the dresser, and I am at the end of it now,' I thought. But I soon discovered that it was not the old painted dresser which I touched, but something carved, as nearly as I could discover with my unskilled finger-tips, with winged things. There were certainly long keen curves of wings which seemed to overlay an arabesque of fine leaf and flower work. I do not know what the object was that I touched. It may have been a chest. I may seem to be exaggerating when I say that it somehow failed or exceeded in some mysterious respect of being the shape of anything I had ever touched. I do not know what the material was. It was as smooth as ivory, but it did not feel like ivory; there was a singular warmth about it, as if it had stood long in hot sunlight. I continued, and I encountered other objects I am inclined to think were pieces of furniture of fashions and possibly of uses unknown to me, and about them all was the strange mystery as to shape. At last I came to what was evidently an open window of large area. I distinctly felt a soft, warm wind, yet with a crystal freshness, blow on my face. It was not the window of my hall bedroom, that I know. Looking out, I could see nothing. I only felt the wind blowing on my face.

"Then suddenly, without any warning, my groping hands to the right and left touched living beings, beings in the likeness of men and women, palpable creatures in palpable attire. I could feel the soft silken texture of their garments which swept around me, seeming to half enfold me in clinging meshes like cobwebs. I was in a crowd of these people, whatever they were, and whoever they were, but, curiously enough, without seeing one of them I had a strong sense of recognition as I passed among them. Now and then a hand that I knew closed softly over mine; once an arm passed around me. Then I began to feel myself gently swept on and impelled by this softly moving throng; their floating garments seemed to fairly wind me about, and again a swift terror overcame me. I struck my match, and was back in my hall bedroom. I wonder if I had not better keep my gas burning to-night? I wonder if it be possible that this is going too far? I wonder what became of those other people, the man and the woman who occupied this room? I wonder if I had better not stop where I am?

"*January 31.* Last night I saw—I saw more than I can describe, more than is lawful to describe. Something which nature has rightly hidden has been revealed to me, but it is not for me to disclose too much of her secret. This much I will say, that doors and windows open into an out-of-doors to which the outdoors which we know is but a vestibule. And there is a river; there is something strange with respect to that picture. There is a river upon which one could sail away. It was flowing silently, for to-night I could only see. I saw that I was right in thinking I recognized some of the people whom I encountered the night before, though some were strange to me. It is true that the girl who disappeared from the hall bedroom was very beautiful. Everything which I saw last night was very beautiful to my one sense that could grasp it. I wonder what it would all be if all my senses together were to grasp it? I wonder if I had better not keep my gas burning to-night? I wonder—"

This finishes the journal which Mr. Wheatcroft left in his hall
bedroom. The morning after the last entry he was gone. His
friend, Mr. Addison, came here, and a search was made. They
even tore down the wall behind the picture, and they did find
something rather queer for a house that had been used for boarders, where you would think no room would have been let run to
waste. They found another room, a long narrow one, the length
of the hall bedroom, but narrower, hardly more than a closet.
There was no window, nor door, and all there was in it was a sheet
of paper covered with figures, as if somebody had been doing
sums. They made a lot of talk about those figures, and they tried
to make out that the fifth dimension, whatever that is, was proved,
but they said afterward they didn't prove anything. They tried to
make out then that somebody had murdered poor Mr.
Wheatcroft and hid the body, and they arrested poor Mr.
Addison, but they couldn't make out anything against him. They
proved he was in the Cure all that night and couldn't have done it.
They don't know what became of Mr. Wheatcroft, and now they
say two more disappeared from that same room before I rented
the house.

The agent came and promised to put the new room they discovered into the hall bedroom and have everything new—papered
and painted. He took away the picture; folks hinted there was
something queer about that, I don't know what. It looked innocent
enough, and I guess he burned it up. He said if I would stay he
would arrange it with the owner, who everybody says is a very
queer man, so I should not have to pay much if any rent. But I told
him I couldn't stay if he was to give me the rent. That I wasn't
afraid of anything myself, though I must say I wouldn't want to put
anybody in that hall bedroom without telling him all about it; but
my boarders would leave, and I knew I couldn't get any more. I

told him I would rather have had a regular ghost than what seemed to be a way of going out of the house to nowhere and never coming back again. I moved, and, as I said before, it remains to be seen whether my ill luck follows me to this house or not. Anyway, it has no hall bedroom.

FACES

Arthur J. Burks

People who know me say that I am insane. Many of them tell me so to my face. They do it jokingly, but in their eyes I read that they half believe it.

But who wouldn't be crazy after going through what I experienced during those dread hours when, huddled in the after cockpit of a wrecked airplane, in the very center of the dread Gran Estero, the pilot dead in the seat ahead of me with his brains dashed out, I sat the hours away with my eyes peering in the shadows of the great swamp?

Perhaps I did not see all the things memory brings to mind from that dread page of the past. For the silver plate in my head suggests many things, added to which there is a long blank in it somewhere during which I somehow won free of the mysterious region of rotting slime and bubbling ooze—a blank that I find myself glad I can not fill. For it must have contained terrible things.

We had taken off from the flying field at Santo Domingo City with plenty of time to spare ere we should be due at Santiago. It only takes a little over an hour, and it still lacked three hours of sundown when we lifted, in a series of climbing turns, into the sunny sky of the Dominican Republic.

But we had forgotten the fog which sometimes rises suddenly in the Pass through the Cordilleras.

We were half-way through when the fog was upon us, shutting us out from the ground below as effectually as though we both had suddenly gone blind, and were hurtling through a sea of mist at more than a hundred miles an hour—quite too fast to think of piling up on some unseen mountainside. I could scarcely see the pilot in the seat ahead. He looked back at me once and shook his head. Then he tried to see the ground below us, as did I. But whichever way we looked there was nothing but that sea of impenetrable white. Even the roaring of the engines was muffled by the density of the fog.

The pilot came back on his stick, and I knew by the way my back pressed against the cowling in rear that he was pointing her nose into the sky in the hope of climbing above the clouds.

Minutes that seemed like hours passed as we continued to climb, on a slant just great enough to keep from stalling, but great enough that I knew we had already cleared the tops of the mountains on either hand. Yet the fog held steadily. It must have been miles high.

Then the aviator got confused. I don't blame him. Though I have never flown a plane I have ridden in planes many times, and know what it means to be caught in a fog or among heavy clouds which shut out the earth. Had he flown straight he might have ridden through the fog; but he did a turn or two in an attempt to find an opening, and lost us completely. Only by the slackness of the belt which held me in could I be sure that we were flying right-side up—which was all I did know!

The altimeter said 10,000 feet, with the needle crawling slowly toward the 11,000 mark! And still the fog.

Finally the flyer held her nose in one direction, at least he tried to, and plunged like a mad thing through the fog. Yet we didn't penetrate the mist wall.

Long after we should have reached Santiago we were still in the fog, still above 8,000 feet, and darkness was settling down upon us.

There was enough gas in the tanks when we left the field to keep us in the air for four hours. My wristwatch told me that we lacked but fifteen minutes of that time! In God's name, where were we? We might as easily have been far out over the Atlantic Ocean, the Caribbean Sea or Mona Passage.

I know now that we came down within five miles of Bahia de Escocesa, which is an arm of the Atlantic, and that, had our luck held for a few minutes more, we might have made a fairly safe landing on the broad shelving beach. Just a few minutes, as time is figured, and a life is lost—while another man lives to hear himself called a madman!

The engine spluttered and died. What a dread silence after the roaring of the motors!

The humming of the wind through the wires and braces told me that we were spiraling downward. We might be headed for a mountaintop or for the open sea and certain drowning—or might be heading directly into the field at Santiago, though only a fool would have hoped for such great good fortune. And still the fog about us held.

The pilot flung his helmet and goggles over the side and looked back at me, grinning widely.

"We're through, kid!" he said. "Ain't one chance in ten thousand of getting out of this with our hides. Let's hope that they find the remains sometime."

I am not ashamed to confess that I could not take it so light-heartedly as this; but then I am not made of the stuff of which flyers are constructed.

The aviator turned his eyes back to the instruments on the board before him, and our spiral continued to the tune of the wind in the struts, a tune that had a sinister meaning, a tune that sang of death uprushing to meet us. The altimeter said 1,500 feet now, with the needle fairly dancing down toward zero.

When we broke through the fog we were directly above a forest of nodding treetops, with scarcely a breathing space before the inevitable crash, which could have been avoided only did a miracle happen and the propeller start whirling again.

It seemed to me that we leveled and seemed to sink straight into the forest, though common sense told me that we must have struck at a speed of not less than ninety miles an hour. We hit the treetops and crashed through.

My head banged against the cowling when we hit, and I remember nothing afterward—until I opened my eyes in the shadows which hold sway in El Gran Estero, and found that the safety belt still held me in my seat. What was left of our right wing was above the dank waters of the vast swamp, while on my left I could see nothing but shadows, and the oozy slime of the dead quagmire. Only the main part of our ship had held together, and this was steadily sinking forward because of the dead weight of the motor.

The aviator was asprawl in the forward cockpit, his arms hanging over the side. I noted that blood dripped from the fingers of his right hand.

I unfastened my belt and leaned forward, swaying dizzily as a terrible feeling of vertigo seized me.

I shook the aviator roughly by the shoulder.

"McKenzie!" I shouted. "Are you bad hurt, boy?"

He was. For, as I shook him, pulling him around by the shoulder, I caught a glimpse of his face. It was not a face, but a bloody smear, with a gaping wound in the forehead. His body was still warm, proof that I had been unconscious but a short time. There was no mark of blood on the cowling before McKenzie's face, and I wondered what had dealt him that blow which had dashed out his brains. Leaning forward carefully I stove to peer down into the cockpit.

When I saw what had done it I all but collapsed. For the forward cockpit had fallen squarely upon the jagged stump of a tree and this had gone through the light fabric and penetrated McKenzie's body in a way that I find myself unable to mention in cold print. He had been dead even before that blood-stained stump had come on through to bash out his brains.

There was nothing I could do for him. And there seemed little chance of saving myself.

I knew that I was somewhere within mysterious Gran Estero, in a plane that was gradually sinking of its own weight—and that I was mighty fortunate to have lived even this long. Besides which I knew that I was badly hurt, how badly I could only guess—as you can do when I tell you that a goodly portion of my skull is silver at the present moment.

How to get out, and what direction to take? How to reach land solid enough to support my weight? In the daytime I knew I could have done it somehow—had I been in full possession of my faculties and my strength.

I studied the swamp around me, but as far as I could see in the darkness there was nothing but oozy morass, into which I should have disappeared within a few minutes at most. Ever the plane seemed to sink lower, as though a great mouth were relentlessly sucking it down.

My head was aching terribly, and oddly colored dots were

dancing before my eyes. Any moment I expected to lose consciousness—and rather hoped that, did I do so, I would never regain it. Death would be easy, and would save me untold trouble and privation, to say nothing of unplumbed suffering.

"Well, why don't you climb out of there and find us a way out?"

I started as though someone had suddenly placed a hot iron against my quivering flesh. In my mind I heard the words, yet I swear that my ears had heard nothing at all. Just an impression that someone had spoken—an impression that had the force of actuality.

The hair at the back of my neck seemed to lift oddly as I whirled and stared into the gloom which was now so deep in Gran Estero that I could scarcely see my hand before my face.

Under a tree with many branches, in the very midst of an area acrawl with the ooze of the vast quagmire, stood Lieutenant McKenzie, boyishly smiling as he had smiled before the crash! From his puttees to his helmet and goggles he was dressed for flying—save for that ghastly red weal across his forehead!

My eyes must have bulged from their sockets as I stared at him; for he smiled again and the smile froze on his lips, never again to leave them. This time when he spoke his voice sounded hollow, and as cold as a voice from the tomb.

"Well, get going! We must get out of here!"

Yet I couldn't move a muscle!

Will you understand why when I mention that the dead body of McKenzie still lolled motionless in the forward cockpit?

McKenzie was dead, killed in a manner that has many times since caused me to waken from horrible nightmares with screams on my lips; yet he couldn't be dead when I could see him, as plainly as you see this page, standing there beneath that tree in the midst of Gran Estero!

I screamed aloud when I found that I could look through that figure under the tree and see the bole of the tree itself. Still that frozen smile rested upon those white lips; still that red weal showed on the forehead beneath the helmet—a red weal that seemed to be steadily dripping, dripping, dripping.

Then I began to laugh, a horrible laugh, in which my body shook so convulsively that I all but fell out of the cockpit into the slime.

And as I laughed the phantom of McKenzie disappeared as though a breath had erased it, leaving me alone in the sinking plane with the dead body for company.

But my laughter was short-lived.

For, looking around again for some possible footing place, my eyes found something in the swam which had at first escaped my notice—a pair of bare feet, with their water-whitened soles just above the surface of the ooze! By some weird necromancy I could look down through the mud to the body which hung upside-down below those feet—the skeleton of a native who had been lost in the swamp.

For some reason my eyes darted back to where I had seen the phantom of McKenzie, to see the figure of a ragged native in his place. This one looked at me out of sunken eyes, and slowly his arm upraised as he pointed to the bare feet, which were all that I could now see of the gruesome thing just outside the plane. A voice issued from the motionless lips of the native—a voice that spoke soft words in gentle Spanish.

"*Si, Señor,*" said the voice, "it is I whom you see there!"

Wildly I laughed, and the phantom of the native vanished as the shade of McKenzie had done at the sound of my maniacal laughter.

Wildly, since I knew that my mind was going because of this weird horror, I searched the jungle wall with frightened eyes.

The night drew on apace, and I will not dwell on it unduly, for I know that in that direction lies madness—madness more mad, even, than is now mine.

For I discovered that El Gran Estero is the trysting place of countless shades!

Out of the shadows they came to stare at me—out of the shadows to stare, to smile coldly, and to vanish—while I laughed at each in turn.

It is strange that I laughed; but I could not help it, for my head ached abominably, and I laughed to ease the pain. Is that a good reason? To me at the time it seemed so; but perhaps I laughed at the faces.

The faces?

I lost count of their vast number, for assuredly there must have been many who have lost their lives in El Gran Estero—whose faces came up before me, for the lips to smile coldly, to smile coldly and to vanish, while others came to take their places.

As it grew cooler as the night drew on, will-o'-the-wisps came up from the ooze. Balls of weird flame, balls that had the shape of faces with smiling lips—all sorts of faces. Faces of negroes, men and women—yes, and children; faces of Dominicans, bronze-burnished by a smiling sun, with here and there the pale, staring faces of white men. Thank God there were but few of these! For I found myself unable to look into their staring eyes. It was as though the white men were brothers of mine, and that I had somehow failed them in the weary search for a way out of the vast quagmire. When they smiled coldly, reproachfully, and I could give them no aid, they would shake their heads deadly and disappear, only to show again down some vista through the tree-lanes, always looking back at me sadly before they disappeared for good.

The saddest of them all was a white woman with a babe in her arms. She stood for many minutes where McKenzie and the native had stood, and her eyes were sunken caverns ablaze with a vast reproach. Her eyes searched ceaselessly the wall of trees, seeking, seeking, seeking. At last she wandered down a lane through the trees, gliding softly away, and once I fancied I could hear the subdued wailing of the babe in her arms. She must have heard it, too, for her head bent as though she soothed the phantom infant. She did not look up again, and, thus soothing the baby with which she must have died, she vanished into the vastness of the swamp. I wondered what man had been the cause of her going to her death in Gran Estero. For there was that in her eyes that told me a man was to blame.

Faces, faces, always the faces! And the dead blackness of El Gran Estero.

When all the shades I had seen, together with a host I had never seen before, some of the latter aborigines who must have gone to their death in the swamp during the regime of Columbus and his governors, came at last and gathered in the ooze about me, to smile coldly and sadly into my face, I must have gone clear out of my head, for that is the last dread happening which I remember.

The plane had sunk so low that slime was beginning to trickle into the cockpit in which I still sat huddled, when the army of shades gathered about me—silent and motionless as though they waited for something. Did they wait for me to lead them out of this never-ending thraldom of theirs? I do not know. I do not know anything about it.

I only know the next thing I remember is that I awoke in a cot in the hospital in Santiago, and that the colonel of the regiment occupying the city was sitting at my bedside. When I opened my eyes the colonel turned to the doctor.

"Can he talk now, Doctor?"

The doctor nodded.

I told the colonel all that had befallen me. As I talked I saw a queer light come into his eyes, and knew that he doubted my story, may perhaps even have blamed me a little for what happened. I wonder why. His questions took a queer trend at the last.

"Why didn't you go back into the swamp with McKenzie and help him salvage the engine of the plane?"

"But McKenzie is dead, sir! He was killed in the crash!"

Again that queer light in his eyes.

"But the natives who found you at the edge of the swamp swear that a man in uniform was with you—a man in helmet and goggles, a man answering in every detail the description of McKenzie. They say he led you out; but that as soon as he had attracted their attention and saw that you would be taken in charge, he turned back into the swamp before they could come close to him. You should have gone back in with him."

But assuredly the colonel must have been mistaken. Perhaps his limited Spanish caused him to misinterpret the reports of the natives. I *know*, in my heart, that McKenzie never left that forward cockpit after the crash into El Gran Estero.

But do I know? After all there is that blank to be accounted for, and often I waken in the middle of the night and lie awake until dawn, wondering.

THE SECRET OF MACARGER'S GULCH

Ambrose Bierce

Northwestwardly from Indian Hill, about nine miles as the crow flies, is Macarger's Gulch. It is not much of a gulch—a mere depression between two wooded ridges of inconsiderable height. From its mouth up to its head—for gulches, like rivers, have an anatomy of their own—the distance does not exceed two miles, and the width at bottom is at only one place more than a dozen yards; for most of the distance on either side of the little brook which drains it in winter, and goes dry in the early spring, there is no level ground at all; the steep slopes of the hills covered with an almost impenetrable growth of manzanita and chemisal, are parted by nothing but the width of the watercourse. No one but an occasional enterprising hunter of the vicinity ever goes into Macarger's Gulch, and five miles away it is unknown, even by name. Within that distance in any direction are far more conspicuous topographical features without names, and one might try in vain to ascertain by local inquiry the origin of the name of this one.

About midway between the head and the mouth of Macarger's Gulch, the hill on the right as you ascend is cloven by another gulch, a short dry one, and at the junction of the two is a level space of two or three acres, and there a few years ago stood an old board house containing one small room. How the component parts of the house, few and simple as they were, had been assembled at that almost inaccessible point is a problem in the solution of which there would be greater satisfaction than advantage. Possibly the creek bed is a reformed road. It is certain that the gulch was at one time pretty thoroughly prospected by miners, who must have had some means of getting in with at least pack animals carrying tools and supplies; their profits, apparently, were not such as would have justified any considerable outlay to connect Macarger's Gulch with any centre of civilization enjoying the distinction of a saw-mill. The house, however, was there, most of it. It lacked a door and a window frame, and the chimney of mud and stones had fallen into an unlovely heap, over-grown with rank weeds. Such humble furniture as there may once have been and much of the lower weather-boarding, had served as fuel in the camp fires of hunters; as had also, probably, the kerbing of an old well, which at the time I write of existed in the form of a rather wide but not very deep depression near by.

One afternoon in the summer of 1874, I passed up Macarger's Gulch from the narrow valley into which it opens, by following the dry bed of the brook. I was quail-shooting and had made a bag of about a dozen birds by the time I had reached the house described, of whose existence I was until then unaware. After rather carelessly inspecting the ruin I resumed my sport, and having fairly good success prolonged it until near sunset, when it occurred to me that I was a long way from any human habitation—too far to reach one by nightfall. But in my game bag was food, and the old house would afford shelter, if shelter were needed on a warm and dewless night in the foothills of the Sierra Nevada, where one may sleep in comfort on the pine needles, without covering. I am fond of solitude and love the night, so my resolution to "camp out" was soon taken, and by the time that it was dark I had made my bed of boughs and grasses in a corner of the room and was roasting a quail at a fire that I had kindled on the hearth. The smoke escaped out of the ruined chimney, the light illuminated the room with a kindly glow, and as I ate my simple meal of plain bird and drank the remains of a bottle of red wine which had served me all the afternoon in place of the water, which the region did not supply, I experienced a sense of comfort which better fare and accommodations do not always give.

Nevertheless, there was something lacking. I had a sense of comfort, but not of security. I detected myself staring more frequently at the open doorway and blank window than I could find warrant for doing. Outside these apertures all was black, and I was unable to repress a certain feeling of apprehension as my fancy pictured the outer world and filled it with unfriendly entities, natural and supernatural—chief among which, in their respective classes, were the grizzly bear, which I knew was occasionally still seen in that region, and the ghost, which I had reason to think was not. Unfortunately, our feelings do not always respect the law of probabilities, and to me that evening, the possible and the impossible were equally disquieting.

Every one who has had experience in the matter must have observed that one confronts the actual and imaginary perils of the night with far less apprehension in the open air than in a house with an open doorway. I felt this now as I lay on my leafy couch in a corner of the room next to the chimney and permitted my fire to die out. So strong became my sense of the presence of something malign and menacing in the place, that I found myself almost unable to withdraw my eyes from the opening, as in the deepening darkness it became more and more indistinct. And when the last little flame flickered and went out I grasped the shotgun which I had laid at my side and actually turned the muzzle in the direction of the now invisible entrance, my thumb on one of the hammers, ready to cock the piece, my breath suspended, my muscles rigid and tense. But later I laid down the weapon with a sense of shame and mortification. What did I fear, and why?—I, to whom the night had been

<blockquote>
a more familiar face
Than that of man—
</blockquote>

I, in whom that element of hereditary superstition from which none of us is altogether free had given to solitude and darkness and silence only a more alluring interest and charm! I was unable to comprehend my folly, and losing in the conjecture the thing conjectured of, I fell asleep. And then I dreamed.

I was in a great city in a foreign land—a city whose people were of my own race, with minor differences of speech and costume; yet precisely what these were I could not say; my sense of them was indistinct. The city was dominated by a great castle upon an overlooking height whose name I knew but could not speak. I walked through many streets, some broad and straight with high, modern buildings, some narrow, gloomy, and tortuous, between the gables of quaint old houses whose overhanging stories, elaborately ornamented with carvings in wood and stone, almost met above my head.

I sought some one whom I had never seen, yet knew that I should recognize when found. My quest was not aimless and fortuitous; it had a definite method. I turned from one street into another without hesitation and threaded a maze of intricate passages, devoid of the fear of losing my way.

Presently I stopped before a low door in a plain stone house which might have been the dwelling of an artisan of the better sort, and without announcing myself, entered. The room, rather sparely furnished, and lighted by a single window with small diamond-shaped panes, had but two occupants: a man and a woman. They took no notice of my intrusion, a circumstance which, in the manner of dreams, appeared entirely natural. They were not conversing; they sat apart, unoccupied and sullen.

The woman was young and rather stout, with fine large eyes and a certain grave beauty; my memory of her expression is exceedingly vivid, but in dreams one does not observe the details of faces. About her shoulders was a plaid shawl. The man was older, dark, with an evil face made more forbidding by a long scar extending from near the left temple diagonally downward into the black moustache; though in my dreams it seemed rather to haunt the face as a thing apart—I can express it no otherwise—than to belong to it. The moment that I found the man and woman I knew them to be husband and wife.

What followed, I remember indistinctly; all was confused and inconsistent—made so, I think, by gleams of consciousness. It was as if two pictures, the scene of my dream, and my actual surroundings, had been blended, one overlying the other, until the former, gradually fading, disappeared, and I was broad awake in the deserted cabin entirely and tranquilly conscious of my situation.

My foolish fear was gone, and opening my eyes I saw that my fire, not altogether burned out, had revived by the falling of a stick and was again lighting the room. I had probably slept only a few minutes, but my commonplace dream had somehow so strongly impressed me that I was no longer drowsy; and after a little while I rose, pushed the embers of my fire together, and lighting my pipe proceeded in a rather ludicrously methodical way to meditate upon my vision.

It would have puzzled me then to say in what respect it was worth attention. In the first moment of serious thought that I gave to the matter I recognized the city of my dream as Edinburgh, where I had never been; so if the dream was a memory it was a memory of pictures and description. The recognition somehow deeply impressed me; it was as if something in my mind insisted rebelliously against will and reason on the importance of all this. And that faculty, whatever it was, asserted also a control of my speech. "Surely," I said aloud, quite involuntarily, "the MacGregors must have come here from Edinburgh."

At the moment, neither the substance of this remark nor the fact of my making it, surprised me in the least; it seemed entirely natural that I should know the name of my dreamfolk and something of their history. But the absurdity of it all soon dawned upon me: I laughed aloud, knocked the ashes from my pipe and again stretched myself upon my bed of boughs and grass, where I lay staring absently into my failing fire, with no further thought of either my dream or my surroundings. Suddenly the single remaining flame crouched for a moment, then, springing upward, lifted itself clear of its embers and expired in air. The darkness was absolute.

At that instant—almost, it seemed, before the gleam of the blaze had faded from my eyes—there was a dull, dead sound, as of some heavy body falling upon the floor, which shook beneath me as I lay. I sprang to a sitting posture and groped at my side for my gun; my notion was that some wild beast had leaped in through the open window. While the flimsy structure was still shaking from the impact I heard the sound of blows, the scuffling of feet upon the floor, and then—it seemed to come from almost within reach of my hand—the sharp shrieking of a woman in mortal agony. So horrible a cry I had never heard nor conceived; it utterly unnerved me; I was conscious for a moment of nothing but my own terror! Fortunately my hand now found the weapon of which it was in search, and the familiar touch somewhat restored me. I leaped to

my feet, straining my eyes to pierce the darkness. The violent sounds had ceased, but more terrible than these, I heard, at what seemed long intervals, the faint intermittent gasping of some living, dying thing!

As my eyes grew accustomed to the dim light of the coals in the fireplace, I saw first the shapes of the door and window looking blacker than the black of the walls. Next, the distinction between wall and floor became discernible, and at last I was sensible to the form and full expanse of the floor from end to end and side to side. Nothing was visible and the silence was unbroken.

With a hand that shook a little, the other still grasping my gun, I restored my fire and made a critical examination of the place. There was nowhere any sign that the cabin had been entered. My own tracks were visible in the dust covering the floor, but there were no others. I relit my pipe, provided fresh fuel by ripping a thin board or two from the inside of the house—I did not care to go into the darkness out of doors—and passed the rest of the night smoking and thinking, and feeding my fire; not for added years of life would I have permitted that little flame to expire again.

Some years afterward I met in Sacramento a man named Morgan, to whom I had a note of introduction from a friend in San Francisco. Dining with him one evening at his home I observed various "trophies" upon the wall, indicating that he was fond of shooting. It turned out that he was, and in relating some of his feats he mentioned having been in the region of my adventure.

"Mr. Morgan," I asked abruptly, "do you know a place up there called Macarger's Gulch?"

"I have good reason to," he replied, "it was I who gave to the newspapers, last year, the accounts of the finding of the skeleton there."

I had not heard of it; the accounts had been published, it appeared, while I was absent in the East.

"By the way," said Morgan, "the name of the gulch is a corruption; it should have been called 'MacGregor's.' My dear," he added, speaking to his wife, "Mr. Elderson has upset his wine."

That was hardly accurate—I had simply dropped it, glass and all.

"There was an old shanty once in the gulch," Morgan resumed when the ruin wrought by my awkwardness had been repaired, "but just previously to my visit it had been blown down, or rather blown away, for its *débris* was scattered all about, the very floor being parted, plank from plank. Between two of the sleepers still in position I and my companion observed the remnant of a plaid shawl, and examining it found that it was wrapped about the shoulders of the body of a woman; of course but little remained besides the bones, partly covered with fragments of clothing, and brown dry skin. But we will spare Mrs. Morgan," he added with a smile. The lady had indeed exhibited signs of disgust rather than sympathy.

"It is necessary to say, however," he went on, "that the skull was fractured in several places, as by blows of some blunt instrument; and that instrument itself—a pick-handle, still stained with blood—lay under the boards near by."

Mr. Morgan turned to his wife. "Pardon me, my dear," he said with affected solemnity, "for mentioning these disagreeable particulars, the natural though regrettable incidents of a conjugal quarrel—resulting, doubtless, from the luckless wife's insubordination."

"I ought to be able to overlook it," the lady replied with composure; "you have so many times asked me to in those very words."

I thought he seemed rather glad to go on with his story.

"From these and other circumstances," he said, "the coroner's jury found that the deceased, Janet MacGregor, came to her death from blows inflicted by some person to the jury unknown; but it was added that the evidence pointed strongly to her husband, Thomas MacGregor, as the guilty person. But Thomas MacGregor has never been found nor heard of. It was learned that the couple came from Edinburgh, but not—my dear, do you not observe that Mr. Elderson's boneplate has water in it?"

I had deposited a chicken bone in my finger bowl.

"In a little cupboard I found a photograph of MacGregor, but it did not lead to his capture."

"Will you let me see it?" I said.

The picture showed a dark man with an evil face made more forbidding by a long scar extending from near the temple diagonally downward into the black moustache.

"By the way, Mr. Elderson," said my affable host, "may I know why you asked about 'Macarger's Gulch'?"

"I lost a mule near there once," I replied, "and the mischance has—has quite—upset me."

"My dear," said Mr. Morgan, with the mechanical intonation of an interpreter translating, "the loss of Mr. Elderson's mule has peppered his coffee."